A
GLORIOUS
THIRD

by Cynthia Propper Seton

A GLORIOUS THIRD

A FINE ROMANCE

THE HALF-SISTERS

THE SEA CHANGE OF ANGELA LEWES

THE MOTHER OF THE GRADUATE

A SPECIAL AND CURIOUS BLESSING

I THINK ROME IS BURNING

A
GLORIOUS
THIRD

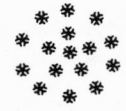

a novel by
Cynthia Propper Seton

W · W · Norton & Company
New York   London

FIRST EDITION

Library of Congress Cataloging in Publication Data
Seton, Cynthia Propper.
    A glorious third.
    I. Title.
PZ4.S4957Gl [PS3569.E8] 813'.5'4 78-14582

ISBN 0-393-08845-6

1 2 3 4 5 6 7 8 9 0

For Nora

Contents

Part One
The Bad Spring (1968)
❋
PAGE 9

Part Two
The French Rebellion
❋
PAGE 121

Part Three
The Good Fall (1976)
❋
PAGE 163

Part One

The Bad Spring (1968)

One

THE Bronx has many mansions; many more than are
probably supposed, and mansions, relatively speaking.
There are quite a number of large family houses, still lying
low beneath the leaf cover of a woodsy hill at the top of
the county, and they don't change hands frequently. This
is not suburbia. There is a subway into Manhattan, and
people with a perch on that hill tend to resist all induce-
ments to come down. Celia Webb Dupont was particularly
successful in this resistance. She was born in one of the
houses on Swift Street at the beginning of the administra-
tion of Calvin Coolidge, she married and had five children,
and was still presiding at the kitchen end of a Georgian
dining room table through the sixties, in spite of civil en-
croachments, erosions, and revolutions; she was withstand-
ing the urban upheaval of those days, if not the intellectual.

It had been a wedding guest's opinion, when Philip Dupont took Celia for his wife in 1947, that he took the house
too, that it was a *mariage à trois*, the Webb house being
the third party. Something pyramidical is thought, geo-

metrically speaking, to be among the most stable of arrangements, which may account for the unusually solid look this
union still had. But of course nothing remains static, although in this particular tripartite arrangement the house,
which was rewired, repiped, and in time recluttered, seemed
to change most. It was a nineteenth-century red stone pile
of castlelike aspirations, with turrets and a crenelated motif,
an offspring of the Smithsonian Institution, greatly reduced
in scale and domesticated by a wide screened porch running
halfway around. At the time of the marriage her friends
weighed in the castle with Celia because she was thin and
pale-colored for a princess, in order to account for her being the choice of a large, confident, ambitious, rather handsome older man: albeit Philip was a commoner.

Now it was an evening in the year of Philip's second
ascendancy, this one professional, when there was a not
notably well-chosen assortment of guests at Celia's table;
her intractable sister-in-law, Marian, for one, and Mary-
Louise Catchpole, a girlhood friend passing through, always
a surprise. Celia would not lightly sever old connections.
The unsevered Mary-Louise had grown up in the castle
next door, and she was interesting for the sociological reason that she had been the only other child whose family had
been going down in the world while everybody else's family
was moving up. Mary-Louise was on a quick visit to her people, lean elderly black-clothed Victorians ending their days
stalking their large mahogany pieces in two rooms and a
kitchenette at the bottom of the hill. Philip, who could not
be a snob since he was a professional champion of the lower
middle classes in the manner of Hubert Humphrey, toward
whom he veered politically—Philip believed that the sociological fact about Mary-Louise was not a good enough rea-

son to keep up the friendship, and he did not see any other reason. He was, however, married to a woman morally constituted to suffer countless people who wished to lay, through the claims of friendship, claims on her time. In the case of Mary-Louise, so careful was Celia not to patronize her, a person of redoubtable certainty, that she was patronized instead. Indeed Celia was half in awe of the wonderful self-confidence Mary-Louise drew from her very insensitivity, and if she, Celia, had not had to defend herself to her husband about this friendship, she might have managed to slip free of Mary-Louise's peculiar tyranny.

"I'm sorry, but I feel I can't vote for any of them," said Mary-Louise, when asked whose nomination she supported. To Celia the implication that M-L (of all people!) deserved something better in the way of a political choice was preposterous. Moreover, M-L had been warned that not only would Philip's brother be there, the head of Heavensgate Press with several political figures on his list, but the historian, very distinguished, K. P. Jacobs. This was a red flag to her.

"Mama has two stickers on her bumper," said Polly, who had come down in her bathrobe to be kissed goodnight. At ten she was the youngest Dupont child, a round little girl with straight brown bangs and the large solemn eyes of a comic. "She has a McCarthy sticker and a Bobby Kennedy sticker, both. My friends say she's mixed up, but everybody wants to win, and I think she's really clever. She has twice as much chance." Polly laughed and was kissed and sent off.

"My wife thinks that Bobby's had an epiphany," said Philip in the courteous tone he used when a woman was the source of an unacceptable opinion. He wouldn't have let a man get away with something like that. No epiphanies.

"I think it's fair to believe people can change," said Celia, without grimacing, managing even to sound almost spiritual. She was one of those who have the blessed nature of a peacemaker by default. They are unable to handle rage.

"Philip's been very fair, very evenhanded," said Tennie about his brother, in a tone granting indulgence, a tone deliberately like Philip's to Celia. If one didn't know Tennie, one might have thought he was standing by Philip; that he meant that Philip, who was now head of the old liberal weekly *The State of the Union*, had been giving courteous attention to Robert Kennedy's entry into the Democratic race. *The State* was not presenting him simply as an opportunist and a spoiler.

"People don't change," Philip said firmly, properly mistrustful of any support his brother felt inspired to offer.

Tennie Dupont was the older of the two brothers, fifty-five to Philip's fifty-two, shorter and very fair. He had a punched-up face about which he decided early to be vain. He told people that he was born with a broken nose and a jaw mislocated in a fierce struggle for birth. The handsome flesh on Philip's face had increased with age and dropped with gravity, and he was losing his dark hair, but he was vain too. And in fact the two brothers, from an outsider's view, were a lot alike, not counting appearance, but they thought of themselves as polar opposites, each rooted roundly in the middle of the other's consciousness, his oldest intractable fact, his most exacting measure, goad, and spur. They could not leave each other alone, although Celia was rarely instructed to include Tennie and Marian on a guest list, beyond Christmas and Thanksgiving. Since there was always something a little forbidden about Tennie, Celia was always a little titillated when he turned up. Meanwhile in town, where each brother was lord of a feudatory, their realms only five office blocks apart, they managed to have lunch together once a week.

Celia was almost forty-five and no longer anticipated parties because of the surprises they might contain, and indeed, was very surprised when there was a surprise. Having Tennie at dinner now gave her a nice tweak. Time and the bearing and rearing of children had changed her from the stringy, nervous, straw-colored girl she had been, to something pink and fleshier, almost voluptuous—the sort of metamorphosis that goes largely unrecognized by a husband. She had taken to enhancing the natural beauty of her hair and then some. Her clothes were becoming, but after a lifetime of being encouraged to put on a little weight, she went over the top and her shirtwaists pulled. Celia was one of those women for whom motherhood was a briarpatch, but as with Brer Rabbit, of a benevolent and ecological order. She lived in a thicket of children and their tangle of activities which were camouflage. It scrambled the data. It gave the impression of a constant maternal supervision. In fact she had become adept at finding private time, slipping out of sight, securing stretches of solitude. People mistook her for the kind of mother who provided her daughters with one enriching experience after the other, but all she really provided was a model and an attitude hospitable to their enriching themselves. She adored her children.

Her dining room chair with its back to the kitchen was the original seat of Celia's power, where she first tasted uncontested authority—after her marriage—and liked it. From it she watched the seasons change across the width of leaded windows opposite. When she was a child there had been draperies, but it was Philip's idea to take them down, and Philip had himself hauled the Tabriz carpet that had been hiding like the purloined letter on the floor of an upstairs room, from which exercise, he claimed, he got his disk. Philip had a grand eye, but for her part Celia failed to inherit the aesthetic covetise remarkable in her forebears for its intensity. She was instead the conservator of the fragments that had escaped the hammer. Previous generations had producd several maniac collectors of heterogeneous or eclectic tastes, most notably her late Great-Uncle Walter Webb, who had made five trips to the Orient, and this house the repository of so many Significant Pieces, in particular Tang. There were none left. Her grandfather had been a bibliophile, and it was from an overlooked folio that Philip found the seven etchings, among them a Bonnard and a Vuillard, which hung now in this dining room above the oak wainscoting and made white rectangles in the dark green jungle of William Morris paper.

The house was ninety-one. It had been bought by Celia's great-grandfather after he had retired from being a sea captain as a place to stow his large, unmarried sons. One eventually and as if reluctantly, at the last possible moment, brought a bride home to it for the purpose of perpetuating the line. The perpetuation was Morris Webb, Celia's father. Women made a very small bow in the family, hardly noticeable enough to account for its arrival into the present. There is no evidence, however, that they were relegated to the backstairs, and to the employment of domestic duties, or rather there is no evidence that there were domestic duties that anybody performed. Even the houseboys did not do them. The rooms and hallways, by the time the child

Celia was running through them, had narrowed almost to warrens, the walls seeming to be supported by stacks of books and papers, large plaster casts of Aphrodite, the Victory of Samothrace, the Apollo of Belvedere among others, reliquaries, caskets, boxes, cartons with coins, fragments, museum periodicals, and catalogues, including Sears and Roebuck, that one or the other of a couple of generations of single wandering souls had picked up and brought home. Under Philip's suzereignty the Webb house alone was rescued and reordered, and by comparison, modestly restocked. It took years. The dining room, with the bonanza of the pictures and the carpet, was his set piece.

This was Friday evening at the end of April in the spring of 1968, which was a false spring in many respects. It was filled with the promise of becoming the nadir of the present cycle of recent history. In the *Times*, Russell Baker wrote, "Many Americans will be disappointed if there is no apocalypse this year," and that was the truth. There were 122 nation-states, and only one had a leader with a sense of human destiny, of moral grandeur. A Herblock cartoon pinned up in Celia's kitchen had a huge de Gaulle looking down upon this ball of earth, with the caption, "—and saw that it was not as good as if he had done it all himself." It was a month after Johnson had been toppled by the peace movement, producing a pause treacherous with hope—and then King had been killed by . . . whomever. It was the day after students had taken five buildings and one dean at Columbia University. In the dining room they were up to eating French bread and cheese with the salad. Celia was an excellent hostess. She was one of the first to serve runny Brie.

"Everybody in New York seems to be buying this Brie now. I guess it's the newest fad," said Mary-Louise, whose job it was to put that sort of thing down.

"Oh, it isn't new, and it isn't only New York. My mother's Brie runs in Kansas City. And in *Vanity Fair* there is a Duchess of Chilton, a Duc de la Bruyere, besides a Comte de Brie. Do you know that, Tennie?" This was young Lily Tucker, who represented one half of the purpose for giving this supper, as against Mary-Louise, who was only there on sufferance.

"Nobody knows that," said Tennie flatly.

"Well, *I* know it because *I* get the cookbooks," said Lily.

Celia hadn't met Lily Tucker before. Philip had asked her. He had a strong inclination to have not only things but people in orderly arrangements, and Lily had been a loose end since he had known her. This was not because of her beauty, but because she was not married, her identifying attribute, from his view; what troubled him, it seemed.

Lily wasn't, strictly speaking, a beauty, because there was a noticeable twist through the center line of her features as though a furious parent had once taken her by the nose before they had set. She had the sort of head Soutine sometimes painted, red-cheeked and rough-hewn, with wild brown hair flying all over the place. Certainly she was not long-stemmed and delicate as her name would suggest, and might better have been called Peaches. In the eyes of a roomful of middle-aged people she looked like a Life Force in a tight red dress with a hem way above her knees,—a high in the history of hems. She was a junior editor in the trade department where Tennie ruled, which accounted for his presence there this night. Another notable thing about Lily was her willfulness. Although she passed for a beauty, and although she was unmarried, she was in single-minded pursuit of professional advancement, although she was a woman.

"There are seven senior editors in our small and *distinguished* firm," she had explained, over cocktails, "and in this respect it resembles the old Brazilian navy where almost everybody could be an admiral instead of a plain seaman. In point of fact, at Heavensgate, they are sea*women*." She had ogled Tennie for a moment, the Old Man, the fleet admiral whose boat she was rocking, and he had returned a steady eye. It had been Philip's intention to rescue his brother from Lily's pursuit.

Now they were eating the Brie and Celia said to Lily, "My mother ran away from Kansas City when she was a young girl."

"Oh, you *have* to. When I went home for Christmas I positively got culture shock! It was so bad when they had parties I had to eat in the kitchen! You aren't going to believe this but when they've finished dessert, my father announces that the women will go into the living room for coffee and the men will stay at the table to drink their brandy!"

"Ah, well," said Celia. "It's just meant to be a pretty conceit, something out of Henry James."

"I think it's insulting! Insulting to women," said Lily grandly, and waved a finger to cross it out. "If somebody sent me off to drink my coffee I'd dump it onto the nearest damask pillow." Lily had a wild smile that made Celia fear for her furniture, and looking for a moment into space, Celia then said, "Terrific! Good for you! That's just what I think too." When the conversation had been rerouted, she slipped off to the living room, and destroyed the evidence, with a beating heart as though what she was doing was not of the most trivial order.

Over brandy and coffee, Celia turned with curiosity to K. P. Jacobs, the historian, a divorced historian, who was Philip's other loose end—Philip had had to go out of his own milieu into the contiguous but discomforting and even alien one of the university to find him. Jacobs wore a navy-blue shirt, a jacket of brown Harris tweed, and a bright yellow tie. There were only white shirts in Philip's drawer. By comparison Tennie, in Oxford tans and blues, looked like a hippie. Without the yellow tie Jacobs might have been lost in the shadows of the wallpaper. Jacobs was a slim, nimble man who looked like a monkey of uncertain age. He had half a head of hair. When he raised his eyebrows an amazing number of ripples rose to his crown. He returned Celia's inviting smile, and taking a sociological interest in her aforementioned evident political dilemma, wanted to know why she would advertise it.

"I like bumper stickers," she said laughing. "I think they are participatory," she added with another laugh, and then becoming a little wide-eyed, she said, "Actually, I'm not drawn by the idea of more Kennedys, but I'm drawn by the idea that people . . . grow. . . . Keats talks about the 'greeting of the spirit.' If one's spirit is prepared to reach out, to greet new experience, reality, one may be deeply altered by the encounter. I like to think that one can evolve, become grander. . . . Anyway, when Bobby was in South Africa, he was speaking at a university to an audience of students who were evidently impervious to what he was saying. They were unmoved. He couldn't stir them. So then he dropped his speech and went to the end of the platform and yelled at them. He said, 'What are you going to

do when you get to heaven and you find that God is black?'
And so that's why I added a Kennedy sticker." Celia finished with yet another laugh. Her laughs were intended to
head off somebody else's laugh.

"It was hardly an original piece of wit, Celia," said Philip.
He didn't laugh and he couldn't be headed off. The presence of K. P. Jacobs unstrung him a little. He was flattered
to have him, and embarrassed by Celia's sounding a fool.

"It wasn't the wit," said Celia to Jacobs. "It was the passion. As if his spirit had wakened . . . and could greet . . .
I suppose if you spend enough time in slums and Indian
reservations it will get to you. But anyway, I think he's becoming something . . . larger. That's what intrigues me."

"Celia, he *has* to court the blacks, he *has* to get that con-
stituency, because McCarthy's got the peace bloc sewn up.
It's a simple political formula," explained her husband in a
patient voice. Their world was the world of thinking people. The only politics was on the left, the only serious can-
didates were Democrats, the only real enemies each other.

"I'm not talking about politics, I'm talking about personal
evolution," Celia murmured, sliding her eyes across Philip
to Jacobs. "I fend against the determinism in psychological
thought, or wherever it crops up. I guess it threatens me."
Celia controlled her manner of murmuring to have it at
once modest and amused. It was her protection against
dragons of which her mother had always been one and her
husband was another.

"Any one of these people will turn 180 degrees every
morning if it will get them on the front page of the *Times*,
or even *The State*." Philip, usually a fair and judicious
dragon, now sounded like Mary-Louise.

Two

K. P. JACOBS had really put Philip off his feed. In the subdivisions of the literate world, Jacobs was a cardinal to Philip's mayor of Boston. And while Philip was paid twice what Jacobs got, in the academic realm money was not the coin, and it was always a question whether Philip, whose pride was in his mind, could have made it up the higher hierarchy. In journalism and publishing, the subdivision in which he at *The State of the Union* and his brother at Heavensgate (named for a lark) were notable representatives, Philip remained unrattled by his regular intercourse with celebrated people. Picture cards were what he dealt in, the reputations of kings and movie queens, the making of artists and writers, senators and even presidents, by paying them attention, and the breaking of them by not paying them attention. Philip had a sensitive conscience, he was circumspect about the uses of power and in particular the use of his own power which he knew was derivative, which derived from his connections with the famous—like their hairdressers, like their wives—but nonetheless and quite helplessly, the sense of his own modest consequence grew smaller and smaller through the years. Celia had said to him not long ago that the liabilities of being an editor were not unlike those of being a surgeon; take their friend Ephraim Davidson, for instance. She said that everybody who walked into Ephraim's office regressed and got childlike. Everybody a surgeon saw in a hospital bed was curled in a fetal position. Inevitably the notion took hold that people in general were naturally craven, and not naturally stalwart the way he was. Philip had agreed it was a problem with Ephraim.

It was in reference to his observation now, when Philip implied that no price was too high for getting the attention of *The State*, that Celia said quietly, "That sounds like a surgical opinion."

Philip darted a cool look at his wife but could not be said to have grimaced.

"Oh, have they finally decided to operate on your mother, Celia?" asked Mary-Louise, who misunderstood the reference and swung the talk to a bank full of shoals. Celia's mother had long lived in the tatty little seaport of La Ciotat in the south of France and had a fever of unknown origin, which had been checked out in the hospital in Marseilles and not resolved. There was disagreement about what was the matter with her. Nothing, was another of Philip's medical opinions.

"No, they aren't going to operate," said Celia. "They're just going to watch her for a while. I was thinking I might fly over with Philip when he goes at the end of June. It would mean taking some of the children . . ."

"There's no point in Celia's going over until something

definitive turns up," said Philip, not for the first time. His mother-in-law, whose relative inaccessibility was usually a convenience, was now an inconvenience.

"Oh, Phil," said Mary-Louise, and her head wagged and her voice hushed out of respect for the sanctities, "she should be with her mother at a time like this."

"For God's sake, M-L," said Philip irritably. "Her mother doesn't even want her. Celia said she was coming over and Agnes said, 'Don't come over, Celia. You'll only upset me.' "

"We all upset our mothers," said Tennie. "And we upset our children in our turn." He and Marian had certainly upset theirs, and this in spite of Marian's having been that sort of mother who had always faithfully turned her full attention to a child in the middle of anybody's sentence.

"Celia's mother doesn't deserve her sympathy, she hasn't earned it. I don't like to see her used this way, that's all," said Philip, but it wasn't all.

"The fact of the matter is, Celia's mother is *fantastic*," Mary-Louise asserted firmly out of her own sense of justice. "She was the most beautiful woman, she could have been an actress! And she had a *fabulous* style. Everybody said she looked exactly like Tallulah Bankhead."

"All her great scenes were in this house," said Philip.

"She made a very unusual mother. Celia looks like her father," added Mary-Louise.

"How old a woman is she?" Lily asked.

"She's sixty-six."

"I've got a terrific manuscript Tennie won't take," said Lily. "*Nurture-Nature and the American Woman*. I can tell you the early years of the century were a poor time here for a middle-class woman to be born. She was reared to bully a few wretched servants and to live a pointless life. It's because unawares she'd been relieved of the single significant role she'd had in a capitalist society—to superintend the transfer of property through the marriage of her virgin daughters. Witness Mrs. Primrose in *The Vicar of Wakefield*, Jane Austen's Mrs. Bennet, and more directly to the point, Mrs. Silas Lapham! Well," she concluded on a note of triumph, "it's taken a long time, but now it's clear there's no money in it, that's the end of virgins!"

"Everybody's going to miss them," said Tennie.

"I don't like this new trend," said Mary-Louise.

"And probably the end of marriage," Lily added.

"Now wait a minute, Lily," said Tennie. "I'm worried about your wiping out our Celia. You're making her redundant, you're doing her out of her rightful expectations, her rewards, all those weddings, all those grandchildren. You know, she has five daughters. She's our own dear Mrs. Bennet."

"Five daughters, yes, I know," said Lily to Celia. "Well, you're lucky you're not Mrs. Bennet."

"Ah, but the golden rewards," Tennie went on. "Those fruitful years of virginity-watching and marriage-arranging and property-negotiating . . ."

"The *primitivism* of what we call Victorian morality!" gasped Lily. "It's not only vulgar, it's absolutely anthropological! I mean I really find it absolutely astonishing to believe that social intimidation could have such monumental power over a technicality as ludicrously trivial as *virginity*. I just think any woman of dignity would be glad to be delivered of the whole humiliating business. Aren't you glad, Celia?"

Celia laughed and said, "yes," with a belying quaver in

her voice, and Tennie lept on her. "Ha," he said, "you really do equate morality with virginity."

"No," she said, confused. "No, that's not my overwhelming question."

"What is your overwhelming question?" asked K. P. Jacobs, the divorced historian.

"Well, I don't really know how to formulate it," said Celia. "But in our world where all the forces seem to be *centrifugal* . . . where everybody in the name of self-realization . . . of freedom . . . is enjoined to get out, break loose, separate . . . divorce . . . where the *nowness* of things is what is most highly prized, most celebrated, well, I guess I seem to be a curious anomaly. I care most about a continuum, for myself, for my family, the sense that we derive from a past, and there is a future, that there is a catalogue of generations, almost Homeric . . . falling leaves . . . almost biblical. I care about history, Professor Jacobs—Peter—but about virginity I don't care a fig." Celia smiled.

Philip grimaced.

"But do you think virginity's been the linchpin that's kept it all going round?" asked Jacobs.

"Well, if it is, I guess we'll have to find another linchpin."

"Celia's father was born in this house," said Philip to Jacobs in a voice a touch reverent. He shared with his wife the need for a sense of historical continuation, the generations unfolding, he the generator, and he had wished he had sons. The children, the Webb house, the ancestral Webbs whom he had borrowed for his own, gave him that sacred plot of ground, that necessary earth from which he drew his strength.

Tennie, spotting the dynastic pretensions in his brother,

said, "If Celia means to track down any ancestors, she'll be well advised to stick to the Webbs. If she goes after the Duponts she won't find us in Delaware. She'll turn up on a chicken farm in Vineland, New Jersey."

"Well, Celia's mother was an aristocrat," said Mary-Louise complacently.

"Aristocrat, my ass!" bellowed Philip. He was not that desperate for connections that he would credit Agnes, his old enemy.

"She was a war bride," Mary-Louise added.

"She was not!" said Celia, outraged by Mary-Louise's proprietary air about somebody else's private life. "My father met her in Paris years later—in 1921. She came from Kansas City. She was a student, an art student!"

"Well, it's the same thing," said Mary-Louise, as though it was.

At this juncture Jacobs raised an arm as if he were pointing to the Red Sea, and said, "I knew it! I remember her! I've had the most astonishing sense of *déjà vu* tonight. I've seen this house. My father brought me here when I was a boy. It was very dark and simply crammed with stuff, and we had to step over . . . I'm sure of it! Paintings, prints, folios, stacked and leaning against the furniture, bad with the good. My father had a gallery on Lexington Avenue, and he knew a lot of private collectors. They called him in when they had something to sell, and sometimes he'd let me tag along. Well, good God, this house! Of course it's tremendously changed, but I know I'm right." Jacobs looked to Celia for confirmation. He was excited by his old memory.

"Yes, surely you are," said Celia in a comforting tone. "They were always short of cash. My poor father spent his life selling off all the things his father and his father's brothers had spent their lives picking up and bringing home. And when they got old, he was responsible for them, he had to maintain them. There was the chronic problem of his taxes and liquidity, and having to find the money so that old Uncle Walter could set out on yet another collecting venture."

"And what about old Uncle Wendell!" said Mary-Louise in an indignant voice.

"Well, he never went anywhere!" snapped Celia, returning the indignation.

"That's right!" said Mary-Louise.

"I remember being hustled through a series of downstairs rooms by two very Edwardian gentlemen," Jacobs continued, musing, not willing to lose the thread of his memory.

"My father and my Uncle Walter," said Celia.

"It was impossible to take anything in. Somebody would flip on a light and point to a piece of sculpture or a painting, stand over you, give you thirty seconds, and then click, and off to the next room. It was like a French *minuterie*. It was like something in Proust. Do you know the soirée at the Guermantes—who own the Elstirs? The paintings?" He had turned to Celia and found her unprepared.

"No, I don't," she said, unwillingly.

"They have a room where they're hanging and they let Proust slip in and he becomes lost in the spell. He stays more than an hour and is late for the supper. Each time I read it I visualize this house and how we weren't given a moment! Afterwards we had tea, and your mother joined us. I can still see her. She was beautiful and young—it's a sepia-colored memory—and she seemed to float all in white across the gloom and flutter down by the tray to pour the tea. It was Irene and Soames to me," Jacobs said, smiling.

"Irene and two Soames," said Mary-Louise.

"Delilah with two Samsons! They had to sell a Corot to buy her off!" said Philip. He was indignant.

"She was worth it!" said Mary-Louise.

Three

PHILIP was seven years older than his wife, and the next morning, a raw and rainy Saturday, he was feeling each of them. Sitting by the library fire like a patient communicant, with his hands in his lap, he was imagining the course that three aspirins must now be traveling, first, round the sharp corners of his left thigh bone, then, drawn upward by his miserable sinuses to hover about his right cheek and eye socket, then across the top of his head and down again to his hips. He had a religious faith in the transcendental circulation of aspirin which was to him the only mysterious good left in this world. Pain called from wherever, and it answered.

The aspirin took care of one headache, but Philip had more. Among other things he was brooding over Hubert Humphrey's pending announcement of his entry into the race for the Democratic nomination. He was sitting now by the phone in the library, waiting to hear from half a dozen people. Celia joined him with the *Times* and made the pages rattle.

"Don't you think Peter Jacobs is a little old for Lily? He must be nearly your age," Celia asked.

"My God! She's been trying to take on *Tennie*, and he's going to be fifty-six!"

"Tennie? Does Tennie play around?" Celia sounded startled. It was her impression that Marian would not have let him.

"You mean a man who was married to Marian would not want to look at another woman? Just as a matter of intellectual curiosity, of aesthetic information? For *art's* sake? After all, he's spent the last two years preparing a new edition of Ruskin!"

Celia's eyes widened to indicate that she was taken aback by such a cross volley against such a broad target, and then said, "I've never read any Ruskin" and went back to rattling her paper.

Philip reviewed Marian. He'd known her from the days in City College when she was the fastest girl in Beowulf to Chaucer, and she'd fallen for Tennie, the senior, when he, Philip, a freshman, had fallen for her. Talk about luck, look what can happen to your smart kid and nifty dresser! She just let herself grow thick and short and mean, and actually paranoid since she'd taken up counseling draft evaders. She thought her telephone was tapped, and that the FBI was staking her out. Good God, suppose he'd married her! And last night she'd turned up looking like Savanarola in some sort of toga and carpet slippers she said came from Nairobi. Well, nobody thought they came from Saks Fifth Avenue.

"Does Jacobs know what he's supposed to do?" Celia asked next.

"Does Jacobs know what he's supposed to do!" He found

it incredible that in spite of the birth of five children and the collapse of all moral standards, his wife remained such a naïf.

"What I mean is, Lily doesn't send out the usual signals. She might disconcert him," said Celia. "When you just look at her, of course . . . well, you don't expect such a *brawny* mind. Anyway, she told me something I think is interesting. She told me the first thing on the list of all the architectural plans of villas the Romans built in Gaul was *baths*. Wouldn't you think hearths? I mean, I suppose it wasn't our fetish about being clean. Probably just the way the necessity for water got transmitted culturally."

"It was *medicinal*. The thing they were after was the mineral content. I don't think you can imagine the wretched physical condition people endured in those days—their stomachs and their livers, not to mention their arthritis and sinus. *I can.* And they didn't have aspirin, poor devils."

Celia was still unconscious of her own physical well-being and not properly grateful for it. For instance, she had not yet got a hypocondriac relationship to the weather. In matters of bodily decline she remained unfeeling. "Well, I think baths must have served their need for sociability. They could dangle their feet over the edge of their pools and talk about politics and love, while believing they were doing some necessary prophylactic good. You know, the way we are willing to sit through improving club luncheon speakers for the company before and after." In fact she was never willing to sit through them.

Philip dismissed the human need for sociability as Celia for aspirin. Each of them, in many of the most personal matters, was an entire stranger to the other: the less intimate the subject, the more they talked about it, and contrariwise. Their marriage was the joining of two natures, the one wanting to please, the other wanting to be pleased. Celia's manner was courteous and of that placatory kind that used to be found in princesses who were in childhood confined to garrets, but is nowadays discovered to be the consequence of an anxious personality. An old definition of courtesy includes "self-suppression in action as well as concrete sympathy." That was Celia. Her courtesy was organic, integral. Philip's was elective and sometimes suspended. It was more aggressive, more pinched or strained, which, according to an older definition is "like gossips neere a stile, they stand straining courtesie who shall go first." He was strained now, but not because he was often a speaker at the very luncheons Celia had people forbearing to sit through. On top of all his public concerns was a private one that left him with a sense of injured innocence. He cast about now for a topic to establish this innocence with Celia.

"You know, this is going to be one lousy month coming up," he said, putting his back to her by turning the logs in the fire. "On Tuesday I talk to that advertising council about using colored models. It's got to be very tactful. If I'm too firm we lose God knows how much in advertising revenue. It's got to be friendly persuasion."

"You mean what kind of blackmail? Get it?"

"They're the blackmailers. They'll just take their money and put it in television. They're doing it anyway. I'm really reluctant to come out of my first audit in sharp decline."

The kitchen phone rang in the middle of the case he was building and Celia went off.

Celia had spent the past year trying to effect this conversion of America to the use of black models and had failed. Of all the do-it-yourself world improvers, she was the most inept. Every time she paid her bill to a Fifth Avenue store she addressed a letter directly to the store president, enclosing her check and asking him whether he would introduce black models into his windows and his newspaper advertisements, and every month he cashed her check and didn't answer her questions. Philip believed that his wife as a political animal—with her peace marching and her doorbell ringing—was so wonderfully diffident, so overlookable, that her opponents remained to the end unaware of the challenge to them that she intended to represent. It was a great pleasure to him to have a wife that well-bred as to be that significantly ineffectual.

Philip had married up, deliberately and ethically, in the finest eighteenth-century tradition. "I make a point," said Joseph Severn, b. 1793, "never to know anyone who is not superior to me in fortune or ability, or some way or other, that I may still be raising myself, or improving, even in moments of pastime." In that spirit through the years did Philip. That his name was Dupont was a piece of luck in America, but Dupont, according to *Le Monde,* is among the twenty most common names in France, the nineteenth in fact. Philip's grandfather had come to this country at the turn of the century, for reasons not recorded, to scratch out a living with his chickens. His father was a typesetter who worked for the old New York *Herald Tribune,* and his mother was an Algerian Jew. Dupont de Nowhere. And in moments of true humility, or useful humility—the speech he would give to the advertising council a latter instance—he would acknowledge to himself that although he crossed the ocean casually west-to-east for a week or so, he was just two generations from a single, solemn steerage crossing east-to-west. For his part, his brother, Tennie, was in no way able to credit Philip's capacity for feeling humble and pronounced their name with the stress on the first syllable, managing to make it sound as common as it was. It was difficult even for the connoisseur to determine which of the two men was the bigger scorer.

Scoring had begun to double in meaning recently with the introduction of Lily, who had been at Heavensgate for a couple of years, trying earnestly to bring her work to the attention of Tennie and failing entirely. Then one day in the fall Lily and her work came to the attention of Tennie. It came by the happenstance of their taking the same down elevator, taking the same right across 53rd Street, the having to chat, the having to stall as they'd reached Pierre's and the casual invitation to join a brother at lunch. Through lunch Philip, who did not for a minute believe Tennie was involved with the girl, pretended to misconstrue their relationship. Tennie, who could not even remember her name, having to mumble the introduction, was amused to play to the misconstrual. All at once it was new theater for them with plots and guiles that are hackneyed enough when other people are the actors but that revived and refreshed their brotherly jealousies and brought each of them upward and out of a slow and involuting depression down which each had felt himself slipping. It was a lucky day for Lily and her work.

The brothers had quickly gotten into their parts. Through the winter scene followed scene. Now it was nearing the end of the second act, during which Philip had decided that Tennie was in earnest and meant to have Lily. Philip was in a passion to stop him. This passion drove him to make Lily an offer, a previously unheard of departure from the way things were done at *The State*, to do a book review. The book was by the woman novelist S. V. Hume, a favorite of Celia's. Lily addressed herself to this task with a youthful contumely also unprecedented at *The State;* and Philip let the review pass. He thought vaguely that the venom had to do with her asking for *Armies of the Night* and his saying it had to go to a man. The review was scheduled for the following issue when the sky would fall down, but he had another week.

Philip got up from his chair and lay down on the sofa, and the cat lept on his stomach, settled himself, and made a warm poultice there. This was comforting and Philip's balled-up mind began to clear a little, and he felt a rush of gratitude for the cat and pity for himself for having only a cat, the least loyally inclined of creatures, to depend upon. Then all at once a brilliant move occurred to him, a sort of multifaceted move he could make that would head off his worst dread—that Celia would read in Lily's review everything that had been hidden in his head—a wily move that would reflect kindly upon his concern for her, and even for her mother! Until this matter of the review there had been plenty of room in his conscience to take on the maneuvering of Tennie for Tennie's (or Lily's or Marian's or anybody else's) sake, because he had a stern sense of his own rectitude and a willingness to recommend, at work and at home, himself as an example, and as long as the ploy was, generally speaking, benevolently intended, it was a safe, if titillating game. With the offer to Lily of the Hume book, however, he stepped out of character, and he was left to marvel how the awkward consequences immediately proliferated. Everything stopped looking innocent. Everything started looking like he was guilty of wanting Lily, the hitherto underlying, unacknowledged truth.

Celia came back to the library and said, "I'm always surprised people don't live by the same terms I do. I thought having M-L last night it was quits, but she's on the way over. She has something on her mind."

Philip, at first alarmed, said generously, "Hell, I don't give a damn. I'll just hang out in here, and you can send in something—some of that veal from last night. It was very very good, and a little white wine, not too cold." And then, dumping the cat, he swiveled to a sitting position, looked at his wife, and said with a full heart, "Listen, my dear girl, I've been thinking about how much you worry over your unregenerate mother. I've decided I'm really wrong to want you to delay your visit until all the girls are married. In fact, go now. If you go now, I'll be here to oversee things, and you won't have all the girls worrying you, and you'll feel better."

"Go now?" Celia said, surprised, and looked at the pictures on the wall as if to make out the reasons why she couldn't, and as she considered, Philip said, "Sure, I'll get you on that Friday night flight. How about that? Gives you the special fourteen- to twenty-one-day rate, and when you get home, well, then I'll go, and then the girls . . ."

"You mean, go by myself without you and the girls?" She had never previously heard confidence expressed in her ability to get even to New Jersey by herself.

"Come on, Paris isn't Newark or Detroit," he said, referring to two cities notable for having lately been torn by riots. And as Friday revealed itself to be the perfect day,

Philip tempered the impatience in his voice and substituted a tone of thoughtful reassurance. "Miss Callahan will take care of the whole business, route you right through to Marseilles. But the real advantage of Friday is that you'll get through Orly before the Peace Conference starts . . . there'll probably be a devil of a crush. . . . And of course, the children will still be in school, so that . . ."

As if they were invoked, the three youngest girls rolled through the door and lined up backs to the fire. They were of a shape to roll, although Harriet, who had just turned sixteen, was suddenly and before their eyes, and while eating the same monumental quantity, turning into a long-necked swan, a metamorphosis observed earlier to have occurred in her older sisters, but still a good trick.

Because they were reared by parents of the generation to whom it was proved scientifically that the more you loved your children the more surely they were destined to have untroubled, happy lives, the Dupont girls had a terrific future in store, although the older girls were giving signs there might be cracks in the system. But as of this rainy April, parental love had not expressed itself in any great display of permissiveness, and these three girls went to their school washed, and combed, and in pleated skirts no more than four inches above the knee. While, however, their childhood was protected as far as their hemlines, they did not have innocent hearts. Harriet and Isobel (Bess) had fasted for peace; and being eaters they were the more distraught when their fastings didn't bring it. Besides defoliation and saturation bombing, they, and even Polly, knew a lot about hippies, tripping, and sex. They went to a very fine school where they were learning firsthand how authority is broken down. So far they were observers.

The two oldest girls, Francesca and Eleanora—Francie and Nell—were at Smith, one a junior and one a freshman. When she was a girl, Celia had gone to Smith, where she was sometimes unhappy; but in the interim the causes of young grief had multiplied exponentially and now the mood on the best campuses was sullen, and the mood of the best parents alternated between compassion and impatience. For Philip these two oldest girls were his surrogate boys. His expectations for them were correspondingly severe, and he regarded their unhappiness as a species of frailty—those liable to it needing toughening. This frailty in Francie, meanwhile, was now manifesting itself in exhausting activity. Although she was matriculating at Smith 130 miles to the north, for which Philip was paying $3,125 per daughter, she had been shuttling back and forth to a bearded boy named Forster, whom Philip called the Woolly Mammoth, and who was a senior at Columbia, which evidently he did not like and had decided yesterday to destroy. Her parents suspected Francie might be in the thick of this battle, and yet her father had not put his foot down. This was because he was as uneasy as the next middle-aged father about what would happen if he did put his foot down: nothing. Still, he had not altogether abdicated, since he had one of those minds able to keep daily track of many interests, much of which was other people's business.

"Well, Harrie, have you gotten through *The Waste Land* yet?" he now asked Harriet, a high school junior, in an admonitory tone.

"Haven't I just!" said Harriet, rolling her eyes, and looking heavily burdened.

"Well, what do you think it means?"

"I haven't a clue!" she gasped, clutching her throat. She was interested in the theater and science.

"That is not an adequate response. Just go on up and read it again," said the stern-browed father.

"Well, if mother could *give* me a clue," Harriet suggested, more tractable.

"Oh, good grief, I'd have to reread it. I haven't read it since . . . well, maybe I'll do that . . . let me have it and I'll look at it this afternoon," said placatory Celia, the first-rate mother.

"Mother will read it," authorized the father. "*And*," he continued in a lighthearted and encouraging voice, "do you know something else? She's going to France! What do you think, girls? Friday! And she'll get old Agnes settled down and off her mind."

"Are you going to bring her home?" round-eyed Polly asked, excited at the possibility of having a grandmother to sit on, but it was misdirected excitement. The grandmother would not come home. The right excitement, she was invited to consider, was the idea of two weeks in the house without a mother in it.

"I don't think Friday," Celia murmured. "Good grief, I haven't . . . I don't even . . . I need time to . . ."

"To what?" Philip asked, with a kindly, encouraging look.

"To think . . ."

"About what?"

"I don't know. About what to bring to read," she said, feeling cornered.

Four

CELIA was at once more and less complicated than her husband. She was designed to be good, good the way her father expected her to be—intelligent, quiet-spoken, well-mannered—good like George Eliot's Dorothea Brooke, whose "mind was theoretic, and yearned by its nature after some lofty conception of the world which might frankly include the parish of Tipton"—or in this case, the borough of the Bronx. But to have passed forty and to have continued to be good three-quarters of the way through the twentieth century, while deprived of "the light of Christianity" that Dorothea saw by, required a lot of trimming of theory, and a great tolerance for irony. Celia trimmed, and irony was mother's milk to her. She was born into an ironic situation, and indeed it seemed to be the motive force of her self-improving spirit. She did not strive to be worthy of the memory of her fine father. She strove to be the source of gratification to a live and uninterested mother whom she seemed to weary by her very excellence. When Celia was eleven, her mother said to her, "I have decided to leave your father but I won't take you with me because he couldn't bear to part with you." A father who couldn't but a mother who could. "You were a plain child, but very loving," Agnes had said casually through the years as if to be plain and to be loving were two amusing attributes, not in her style. And it was no doubt unmotherly of Agnes to speak with such candor to her daughter, but curiously, and overall, it had the useful effect of sending Celia off into the world intent upon making herself more interesting and less plain.

The belief that marriages are made in heaven has been superseded by the more scientific assurance that they are actually made in the unconscious, but insofar as it was offered for a comfort, this newer view was destined to have a short vogue. The Duponts might have observed any number of marriages they knew, shaken their heads over the seeming incompatibility of the principals, and assumed that buried, elemental needs were answered. Now, at the periphery of their lives, a number of separations and divorces were occurring that reopened the question about the aptness of the answers to the buried needs. Celia and Philip were themselves becoming exceptional and might even have been objectionable in what looked like monogamous complacency, if their situation had not been universally understood by the many people of psychological insight who cared about them. Celia was excused because her friends understood that the very absence of stability in her childhood caused her to value stable family life at any cost. They could excuse her, and it was a comfort to them. Philip's condition, no less confidently interpreted, was assessed from two vantage points, professional and private; the two separate lives that sort of man leads, which are tied by a ribbon of crucial little dinner parties. At *The State*, where he had moved up from the ranks, he was respected, his authority feared, and at sentimental moments, in particular since he'd lost his hair, he was even loved. But he was known as a reserved man who opened up only in private life. In private life he didn't open up. People who saw Philip *en famille* believed he was one of those men for whom work was his mistress, which went a long way, they thought, to explain the success of his marriage. By grounding in this way the causes of such a rare phenomenon as marital felicity, it could be forgiven.

Notwithstanding this felicity, Celia and Philip were now enduring a tension of considerable stress for them over the most intimate issue of them all: the choice of a Democratic presidential candidate. Philip may justifiably have been called evenhanded, since editorially he did not exacerbate the Kennedy-McCarthy conflict, but his intention, Celia suspected, was to throw confusion into their ranks so that Humphrey would emerge the winner. Celia's two stickers, on the other hand, were not an attempt to throw confusion, but an offer of reconciliation, a protest against brotherly slaughter, and in Philip's view, of an efficacy on the order of her integration efforts with the president of B. Altman & Co. This primary division—as in presidential primary—was representative of the fault in their union—as in San Andreas Fault.

For his part Philip was, flatly, not a psychological-minded person, not self-probing. As an example, in respect to Celia's family, he was unswerving in his devotion to the legend of her fine and noble father, Morris Webb, whom he had known only as a dying man. Morris Webb was good and Agnes Webb was bad. A lot of emotional energy may have gone into denying the ambivalence he had felt toward his own parents, but nobody has to be ambivalent about other people's parents, and he wasn't. It had been simple for him to see that Agnes, who had walked out on a decent husband and above all a young child, did not merit the normal expressions of solicitude. And Celia should not express them.

Logical, not psychological, was his kind of mind, a proclivity no doubt confirmed by his law school training. He entered the most lightweight of his daily encounters by the adversary system of procedure, as though there always lurked behind even a casual observation an argument to demolish. Celia's father had this characteristic too, which may be evidence, after all, that the unconscious, if it hasn't actually succeeded in getting its needs met, settles for traits of personality that are familiar and safe, the devil it knows. It was a reflex in Philip's nature that he could not just enjoy a theory—Lily's about the Roman baths, for instance—or entertain a proposition—that Celia should visit her mother. He must reveal the flaws in it, or improve the implementation of it; he must deny it or dismantle it. Conversation with Philip tended to be a Socratic dialogue in which he was always Socrates.

A Democratic party united behind HHH will win.
A fragmented and rancorous party will lose.
Therefore those people who support McCarthy or Kennedy
    will elect Nixon.

And he said to Celia in one way or another twenty times:

Mary-Louise is a dull and vulgar woman.
(You are a patsy.)
Whatever she has to say is of no interest to you.
Whatever you have to say is no profit to her.
      Therefore, cut her off.

But Celia could not cut off anybody and was without syllogistic resources with which to defend her position. And as it turned out at lunch on this particular day, she was interested to hear what M-L had to say, and was furthermore a considerable profit to her guest, four thousand dollars worth of profit. And all this without M-L's departing from her usual complacent manner, beginning with her arrival and not ringing first, just walking in.

"Come on in," said Celia, once again wasting a little sarcasm on Mary-Louise.

"Come on in, Mrs. Catchpole," repeated Bess, one in a family of stand-up comics. "The opera is going to be on in a minute. Faust. I plan to listen to Faust and read Thucydides at the same time. I think it will be a good combination, all that slaughtering on the one hand, and all that shrieking on the other," and she giggled her way upstairs.

M-L was wearing jeans, not out of being in the height of fashion but because of having gone back to the soil, or near to it, from the beginning of Cal's ministry. They lived now in southern Vermont with their two boys and a girl, cats, dogs, and a horse, but no chickens, and therefore, it seems, no egg money.

"I'm not going to be subtle," M-L warned unnecessarily. "I'm coming to you with the age-old problem: money. I'm going to tell you right out, I'm not going to beat around the bush, it's four thousand, and you can't get a loan like that without your husband's signature. I want to go after a certificate in money and banking. It takes two years —from the community college—and four thousand will do it."

"Well, of *course* I'll . . . but why wouldn't Cal sign?"

"I thought you'd wonder about that. But the fact is he's a very complicated individual, very proud, and he doesn't believe a wife should work—I would really like to get a bank position, you see—not but that what the parish expects from me isn't work, my God, but he's touchy . . . and right now . . ."

"Oh, well, I didn't mean to pry and of course I'll be *glad* to."

"It won't be a bad investment. You'll get it back. You won't have to worry about *that*." She paused and added, as though with difficulty, "And I want to thank you. But you know, Ceil, you're a little spoiled, because you've only had to look out for yourself. First your father ran everything and then Phil. You've been very lucky the way things fell into your lap."

Celia's jaw set and her knee jiggled under the table and she searched in anger for an answer when fragments in her mind all at once came together, and she remembered walking back from school with Mary-Louise. They were talking about *The Waste Land*, the English assignment.

"What did you think?" Celia had asked.

"I thought it was boring," said the awful Philistine.

"I thought it was wonderful," said the awful liar.

This recollection seemed so telling to Celia that it turned her anger almost to amusement, almost to tenderness, and

Mary-Louise may have been responding to her softened expression when she said, "I might as well tell you the whole thing. You know an attractive pastor, well, I guess you could say it's the hazards of the trade, but they always have some woman crying on their shoulders . . ." She allowed Celia a moment to understand the inferences.

"You mean Cal has other women?" Celia was shocked. She found it incredible that any woman would not shriek if he touched her.

"You can say it's the price you pay for being married to an attractive man. And of course a real man, especially when he gets to that certain age . . . Phil may be different . . . but anyway, what can you do? It's just nature. It's just one of those things you have to live through."

"Well, what about a normal woman?"

"Well, she's got a choice. She can sit and suffer, or she can try to get some of her own back."

They both thought about this quietly although differently and then Celia said gently, "I hadn't any idea, M-L, that you weren't happy."

"Oh, I don't think of myself as unhappy. I think I just have the ups and downs of normal life."

"And you don't want to . . . leave Cal?"

"Leave Cal? I *love* Cal! I knew from the moment I met him that I could never love anybody else."

Celia found she was made unsteady by a wave of envy, and then M-L added, "Besides, I would never give him the satisfaction."

Afterward, when the check was written, M-L asked, "Are you going to tell Phil?"

"Why do you ask such a thing?" Celia said sharply.

"You know," M-L said, "you're a big snob. Well, I'm a snob too. I don't want to look like a failure any more than the next person." That was her parting shot.

When she left, Celia went upstairs to her room to read *The Waste Land* and cheer up.

Five

WOOLGATHERING was so integral a part of Celia's nature that she was rarely found sitting alone without knitting in her hands. Palpable reality, however, had always been Philip's territory. Fact and fancy were clearly distinguishable to him, and he was often called upon to point the difference up for other people. This facility made him a proficient in that most factual of all worlds, newspaperland, but in the realm of romantic fancy he was like Pinocchio at the carnival. Because of inexperience, because he hadn't the usual lifetime of dealing with fantasy, he found his mind swinging across a great hyperbola, where at the one end he discovered himself a shocking scoundrel and at the other a dear beguiling boy. At either end he remained confident in the management, and therefore he was really very surprised that of all people to turn up together at the door at five this very afternoon were Tennie, Jacobs, and Lily, ready for a drink—although he had set them all in motion. That is, while he had rearranged his intentions concerning a match between Lily and Jacobs, they had failed to intuit counter-manding instructions.

Tennie and Lily and he had been at lunch one day a couple of months back when Tennie had mentioned, inno-cently and *en passant*, that he had been looking through jacket designs, all unsatisfactory, for a paperback they were reissuing, a book on medieval Venice by their mutual friend Jacobs. That was how the idea of Jacobs got into Philip's mind. Tennie had put it there. Time passed, and Philip had made a suggestion here, a suggestion there, but nobody took them or felt obliged to report back to him, and mean-while he became so familiar with his conviction that Lily and Jacobs were well-suited and must be mated that he set up the dinner party. By the time of the dinner party he had begun to change his mind about the suitability, but in any case last night he had returned to the object of the book jacket with no particular intent. It seemed progress had not been made there.

"Why, the place to come is right up here at the Cloisters," Philip had said to Lily, off the top of his head. He was a man with good ideas to spare.

"It's not her book," said Tennie. "It's not a trade book."

"I've never been to the Cloisters," said Lily. "I must make that a project."

That is to say, that Philip brought up the Cloisters with-out the least intention that this should be a suggestion for a rendezvous, and they took it.

And they were one and all grateful.

"Lily had a marvelous time," said his brother in kind acknowledgment. "And she had this great idea for Peter's jacket. It was a woodcut after Giotto of a woman who'd hanged herself. Really fetching."

"It was called *Despair*," said Lily with strong feeling. "It was an illustration of the *sin* of *despair*."

"She's got a real taste for the deadly sins, you see," said Tennie.

"Well, I admit it wasn't a good idea for the book," said Lily, "because the Venetians were temperamentally quite hopeful, and with good reason, isn't that right, Peter? But what I found so interesting was that they looked with *contempt* upon somebody in despair, whereas we look with compassion. Of course, as Peter says, the Church didn't want people opting out. They'd have lost all their communicants."

"There must be something medieval about me," Celia murmured, fresh from reading *The Waste Land*. "Despair makes me angry . . . sometimes. It seems too self-obsessed, as if one's own sensibility were especially precious . . . more precious than anybody else's . . . *too* precious . . ." She trailed off.

"Well, cheer up, old girl," said Tennie. "You'll be glad to hear that we'll probably use Giotto's *Hope* for the cover, although she looks to me like Isadora Duncan trying to glide with fifty extra pounds."

"In any case, we had an absolutely wonderful afternoon," said Lily, specifically to Philip, as if their pleasure were owed to him. "Peter is magnificent. He knows all the symbolism. He's particularly enjoyable about martyrs. He says it takes one to enjoy one. Did you know that when St. Stephen is being stoned St. Paul is always in the corner holding his cloak for him?"

"Very nice," said Philip.

"Well, anyway," Lily said, turning from Philip to Jacobs, "I thought it was just great—and how Mary's rejected suitors break their wands across their knees, *so* disappointed. I'd love to go through Europe with you." She had raised a knee to break a wand in the most attractive display of chagrin.

"There aren't such cozy cloisters there. No central heating, you know," Jacobs said, sounding modest, as though he would like to take her but couldn't absolutely promise to deliver.

"I can't think of anything more satisfying," said Celia, "than to trail through Europe with somebody who knew the iconography."

"Well," said Philip, who'd heard enough about their afternoon, "Celia's decided to go to France on Friday, get her mother settled. Let's see, didn't you say, Peter, you were off to Paris yourself?" In a wonderful moment Philip saw that even more brilliant disposition of the principals might be effected by dispatching Jacobs to the south of France with Celia.

"Not Paris, no. I'm going to be spending the year in Bergamo."

"Oh, I don't think Friday," said Celia uneasily.

"Where did you say your mother lived?" Peter asked.

"She lives in La Ciotat," Philip answered for her. "It's about seventeen kilometers east of Marseilles, where she has a choice view of oil tankers in drydock, and she eats squid. First she paints them and then she eats them. Do you know that marvelous song Bea Lillie sings?" And he jumped up, flexed his wrists, and began, in a most elegant, clowning British accent to sing, " 'She heard a voice within, saying paiiint Miss Bea-aaa-trice, paiint—' Do you know it? Her "Still Life"?

Then I bought me an apple
I bought me a peh-ah
I placed them with ceh-ah
in a pot.
I stared at their contours
For roughly two oo -eurs
Then decided to eat the lot!"

They laughed. Lily Tucker did not know who Beatrice
Lillie was, nor that there was room for two lilies. Philip and
Tennie vied with each other to reassure her, singing examples. They were of an age in which Noel Coward had been
once and for all their definition of soigné. Celia thought
they were two frauds but Philip much the better at it. He
had a music-hall side to him, kept usually in the wings, the
part of him she'd fallen for originally. He was light on his
feet as some big men are, and he was even funnier these
days with a stomach and a bald head, his long lean arms and
legs swaying off to the right, then off to the left, a cross between a crab and a blowfish, but easy, quick, and graceful.
He did the "Zither Song" picking the zither notes out on
the piano, and "Love Came to Mrs. Wentworth-Brewster,"
and the children came down at their father's first bellow.

Celia, who had discovered herself to be uncheered by her
reading of *The Waste Land* and had gone gloomily to greet
her unexpected guests, was restored altogether to good
humor. A pleasant disposition was expected of her; small
allowance was made when her mood was bad. Now as she
watched Philip take over, easing Tennie to the side, and she
listened to the familiar lyrics, she thought, amused, that for
the first time she was hearing the real joke of them, the joke

of aging sensuality, the gray joke. Afterward she said, "You know, I really never caught it before, but talk about having to *be* one to *know* one, the funniest thing about these songs is their underlying . . . sort of *desperate* defiance about . . . well, anyway, *middle age.* You know, with her husband's funeral cake in her mouth, she says, 'That's done! It's time I-Had-Some-Fun!' and off she goes to the Isle of Capri, lands up in a bar with a lot of young men who are delighted to be available to her, and she's . . . *very happy.*"

> "Sheer ecstasy at once produced a
> Wild shriek from Mrs. Wentworth-Brewster,"

sang Philip once again, an illustrative chorus.

"It's just a matter of reaching middle age, I guess," Celia said. "Handy to know about those young men in Capri," she added smiling.

> "Hot flushes . . . of delight suffused her,
> Right round the bend she went,
> Much to her astonishment . . . "

sang Philip, who did not trouble to follow his wife's train of thought.

"Darling, those boys weren't there for aging widows," said Tennie, but nobody pursued that line of wit. Finally young and merry Philip was exhausted and let go his hold of the center, and the others began to talk, not very firmly, of going home, when Francie, the Smith-Columbia commuter, was all at once standing in the archway, dripping wet.

"Francesca! What the hell are you doing home again?" said her father for a welcome. Francie gave a defiant look to his chin, said how-do-you-do all around, explained that she could use a lift to the bridge for the 9:15 bus, and asked if she could speak to her mother a moment.

Her father, with only enough energy left to wave a finger, said to her mother, "For God's sake, see that she gets into some dry clothes."

Celia followed her daughter upstairs with a sinking heart. In their last serious conversation at Christmas Francie had said, "Mama, when do you think a woman knows she's ready to have a love affair?" Celia, who believed the horse was already through the barn door, had replied, "When she does not have to share the experience with her mother." Now, while she assisted her daughter at her toilet (she took the wet jeans down to the dryer) she thought she was about to hear what M-L would call another age-old problem. But it was not exactly.

"I just want you to know I'm finished with Forster."

"You were down there through all this business?"

"It was awful. It was the least exalting experience in my whole life." She was twenty.

"Was he hurt?"

"No. But when you see somebody you love under fire and he is . . . *ignoble* . . . a child in a tantrum! You've got to stop thinking of him as a man, mama."

"All right." Forster was twenty.

Francie, in the throes of despair, talked about her anguished decision and cried, and her mother in the throes of relief, comforted her. All these years she had been waiting for her children to grow up so that she could stop worrying about them. So far, and perversely, it seemed they were intent on worrying her more the older they grew. After a while Francie left the particular for the general and said soberly, "The worst is that I've got this awful premonition that the one thing I'm not capable of doing is *staying* in love. I just doubt very much that if I knew a man intimately over a period of time I wouldn't be turned off."

"Intimacy is always a very delicate matter," said Celia, "and in love, in marriage, the great problem is to provide *space* . . . " a theme she developed, and then finally she said, "People tell you today to talk everything out, but there isn't any formula, and I don't see how you can get through without tact and kindness, without overlooking a lot . . . papering over . . . no matter how grand a man is."

Francie set her jaw, looked at her mother, and then said, "I don't want to hurt your feelings, but the entire family pussy-foots around daddy. And you arrange that. Even when you get your way you preserve the illusion that it was *his* way. Well, I'm not going to do that for any man. I really believe in equality!"

Downstairs the guests not, evidently, having engagements to rush off to, stayed on, encouraged, as they thought, by Philip who said, "Don't go yet. Celia will be down in a minute." But in fact Philip was in a fever to separate Lily out, not buy the lot. He said, "Why don't we have some Chinese food sent over?" and then he said, "I guess you can't because Marian's waiting for you, Tennie," and then Lily said she'd go along with Tennie too because he was "her ride." Peter stayed, the now superfluous Peter. He lived near the bridge and could get a lift home easily when Celia took Francie to the bus. Philip didn't even like Chinese food.

At the end of the evening, when Philip and Celia were alone again, Philip raised his chin, lowered his eyelids, and asked, "Doesn't Smith have any residence requirements?

You see what they're doing at Barnard." At Barnard they were thinking of throwing out a student because she was living off-campus with a boy.

"When I was at Smith we were allowed three cuts a class, and we had to check in at 10:15 on weeknights. There were a hundred petty regulations. They were what our outrage focused on. Now it's focused on bombing Asian peasants."

"Well, dearie, I take your point. But I don't know that the quality, or let us say the *efficacy*, of an educational institution is to be measured by the *incidental* outrage cultivated by its students. In any case, she can tear up Smith. Why should she come down here and tear up Columbia when she can tear up Smith? After all, I paid for Smith. And where does she spend the night when she's down here? I'd just like to know where she spends the night? She doesn't come home!"

"Well, I don't know where she sleeps, but actually, Philip, it isn't a matter I have much control over."

"Well, you can talk to her, of course."

"Well, I do talk to her."

"What do you say?"

"For goodness sake, she's twenty. I can't say, 'Be sure and remain a virgin until you're married.' After all, when I was her age I thought being a virgin was practically medieval. It was so unsophisticated, a great embarrassment. Don't you remember how gleeful I was when we . . ."

"That was different! We were going to get married."

"You misremember my past, old boy. I was very anxious to lose my virtue. Very anxious. And I can't in good conscience warn my daughter . . ."

"Well, there's no point in being flippant about it."

"What do you think I ought to say?"

"I just don't like all this sleeping around. I think it's coarsening, it's debasing . . ."

"For boys too?"

"*Yes*, for boys too. I don't cross out a circumspect . . . affair now and then . . ."

"For girls too?"

"What is the matter with you, Celia? Why are you so waspish about this? Do you want to see Francie or Nell up there in one bed after another?"

"I know," she sighed. "I know. But there isn't any language, any folk wisdom from which a mother can draw to recommend to her daughters, in all sobriety, a . . . circumspect affair now and then."

"What the hell are you talking about? Circumspect affair now and again!" And then for a few seconds he had a glimpse of the fourth of July, and he saw the grant of an amazing permission that might be extended to himself. But that show of grace left a black sky as quickly as your usual Roman candle. Philip could not trade off at the expense of his beloved Francie. And so his elation was followed by a confusion of emotion, a sense of sacrifice and defeat ("Let's go to bed," he said. "No, I won't yet."), and then frustration.

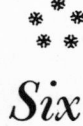

Six

Down the single track of mind they went, two rails;
Philip the people manager and hundred-friended Celia.
Through this present stretch they were as incurious (Philip)
and as unprying (Celia) in regard to each other as ever,
because it was in their characters to be so. When Philip
sulked alone on his side of the bed that night, overstimu-
lated, undersatisfied, angry, as though it were a matter of
a layout he had asked for that wasn't there, and indeed that
was the matter, he never for a moment doubted that his
wife was essentially the same modest-minded and frail girl
he'd married, only fatter. He believed she would be forever
unaware of the enormous exigencies men experience, and in
fact, it would have appeared to him unseemly in the mother
of his daughters to be concerned about the surges of youthful, frenzied lust of the male, unthinkable that she might
be liable to such a surge, more unthinkable that she might
be the object of one. Her ingenuousness made him impa-
tient, but nevertheless he wanted an innocent wife, and indeed, the permission he gave his own thoughts to stray was

predicated on his belief in her unerring taste for minding the hearth. Tennie, he supposed, wanted an innocent wife, but Philip would not have put his money on the old Marian he once knew. He did not think the less of Marian for such a past, he thought the less of Tennie. It was the sort of moral man Philip was: not so much hypocritical as unreflective, and therefore in his way innocent too.

It was to his innocence that Lily of the many red dresses had at one lunch directed a Marxist indictment, in her excited, clear-eyed, wild-haired, arm-flailing way. "We've got an author," she said, "who's doing a *fascinating* piece on the evolution of the mores of capitalist society as it has to do with marriage. You see, in the old days, the husband and wife used to hoe happily side by side, but with the advent of the industrial revolution husband and wife are significantly separated. The man has to *leave* the house and go to an office and be competitive, and cut throats, and do usury, and whatever else in contradiction to Christian teaching. And this leaves the moral part of his nature *too starved*, you see. And so the imbalance is corrected by having the *home*, the wife and children, be the repository of Christian virtue. He's split in two, don't you see, and can be ruthless and successful at work because his home is where his moral self is, his cultural and moral being. It accounts for the woman being stuck, you see, holding the moral bag."

"Well, it's a quite charming notion, but it's wrong, my dear," Philip had said, allowing himself to take her hand for the moment, to signify that he was wiser. "All your author has to do is read Engels and he'll see . . ."

"She'll," said Lily.

"She'll see that everybody was ground down in the mills together. Man, woman, and child. Couldn't have been more than 5 percent had an office to go to!"

"If that isn't a refutation, I don't know what is," said Tennie languidly, and with a look at Lily that was conspiratorial.

"I love him," said Lily enthusiastically, meaning Philip. "He's so unbelievably nineteenth century! I mean he really thinks women are meant to be innocent *by nature* and men aren't!"

Lily's Marxist author might have found in Celia an almost banal illustration of what innocent little girls were made of in the ripe capitalist society between the wars. Celia grew up with a curious lot of illusions, and more curious, she was not *dis*illusioned by the sequence. It might at first seem remarkable and lacking in causation that she passed through a childhood virtually ignorant of the existence of cancer, divorce, narcotics, psychosis (or even neurosis), homosexuality, or indeed, plain sexuality, although she was not twelve when that remote presence, her mother, left the house for good, and by the time she was twenty-four her two great uncles probably, and her father certainly, had died of cancer. It may seem so, but her childhood was not exactly an exercise in denial, a denial that life is uncertain, that in reference to the building on shifting sands her castle was the one mentioned, that households can fall apart, it was more a lesson on how to fall apart well; not in the fact, that is, but the style.

It was an understated style. All the unpleasantness went on at the end of corridors, behind closed doors, further muffled, no doubt, by wall hangings and carpets and the sheer quantity of objects that absorb sound. Time and again down a dark hall hurried a white nurse like the White Rabbit, but Celia's room was in the west bay opposite, above the big yellow kitchen, with shiny Sophronia in it, and the porch full of morning sunshine. That was Celia's own charmed territory, her safe space, where she heard well-bred, reassuring versions of events.

"Well, yes, dear old Wendell is dying," said her father reasonably when he held out his hand for a walk to the sickroom. "After such a long life a man is bound to grow very tired body and soul. And nature makes an interesting use of illness people often overlook. She makes a person wind down and be ready to stop—be glad to be finished." This sort of explanation was comforting if improbable. It had eased the death of her dear grandfather; her grandfather, the sea in his blood, who every Independence Day, rain or shine, had taken her on the Hudson River Day Line to Poughkeepsie and back to celebrate the Glorious Fourth.

It did not obviate all anxiety. Celia had loved her Great-Uncle Wendell. He had read her her bedtime story when she was little, always the same story. In fact always only the first half of "The Brementown Musicians."

"Not again!" he would say. "*Yes*, again!" And she would squeal and giggle. "Once upon a time there was a rooster who minded the hencoop but because he was getting old the farmer was planning to have him for Sunday dinner. So he ran away . . ." ". . . there was a cat who had chased the family mice for years but because he was getting old the farmer . . . so he ran away . . ." ". . . a great mastiff, who had guarded . . . but because he was getting old . . ." ". . . a donkey . . ."

Celia had been at once a worrier who picked at her food, and a cold-catcher, and at the same time an affectionate and obedient child, available to the family elders, including Sophronia and the houseboy of the moment, to be loved. As she grew to her majority, her good behavior was internalized in the usual form of an active conscience, but also in a capacity to accommodate her polite mind to the most impolite information. This caused her, for instance, to regard the current rebellion of the young, the dropping out, the gurus, and even the eruption of violence at Columbia, with sympathy, generally speaking. But to her own children she had observed (too often, evidently), "When one loses an illusion, one doesn't carry on about it. One doesn't take it as an excuse to duck out of life."

As to sex, through a long period of absorbed mothering, much of it corresponding with the Eisenhower years, her capacity to adjust her mind to the imaginative new achievements in this field was not seriously tested. But recently, with the advent of permissivism, everybody was tested, and friendly Celia, Philip would have been surprised to know, was kept up to date on all the record-setting by a lot of friendly people.

Getting the lift from Celia this Saturday evening Peter Jacobs was friendly, for instance. First Francie had to be left off at the bus for Massachusetts for which journey she was in costume suitable for a trek through a swamp. Celia was not in all respects an ideal mother. She could not be relied upon to withhold comment.

"When you go on a trip like this, when you go into any public place, it seems to me to be so *disrespectful,* so contemptuous, really, of all the other people, when you don't dress for the occasion. Everybody's morale is sapped, it seems to me, by this sort of *defiance.*"

"Well, mama, I'm just going to tell you something this fellow told me the other day. A friend of Forster's. He works in the barrio, he works with these young Puerto Rican kids, you know? Well there was this graffiti? It said, 'Don't get dressed because you're not going.' "

This was the sort of answer the mother was getting lately.

"I understand that Sartre's stopped wearing collars and ties," said Jacobs, who was accustomed to parry the anger of the young. "Not entirely for political reasons," he added. "He seems to find them uncomfortable."

"Do you actually know Sartre, Professor Jacobs?" Francie asked.

"I used to see him around. Before he switched gear, so to speak."

Ordinarily Francesca did not admire rank, but she was not a good zealot and enjoyed the idea of meeting a man who not only knew Sartre but knew what he wore. She went off to school in better spirits for it.

And that left Jacobs alone with Celia, who did admire rank, and who wanted, in a brief, casual, clever way to distinguish herself in his mind before they got to his door. Words did not come. Like Philip she was put out of kilter by that touch of modesty an outsider may feel before somebody inside the university world. Insiders do not feel this modesty. Jacobs lived in Morningside Heights, a neighborhood that was in fact on the eveningside of the city, named by the people of New Jersey, perhaps, in one of their Sisyphean efforts to establish their own centrality. They drew up before the lighted marquee of an Italianate old apartment building with Celia feeling thwarted in having failed in forty blocks to make herself intriguing.

Jacobs did not notice her failure and did not open the door and get out. It was pouring. He settled himself kitty-corner against the seat, and with his arm stretched along the top began to play an overture to Celia on the fringes of her scarf. He had the sort of fingers that worked like tendrils when he was near a woman. For Celia's part, as men had not found her of sensual interest until lately, she was quite engaged by their surprising change of attitude. She could not easily relinquish the amazing pleasure it was to be at the center of attention in a group not made up of her own children (and in this respect she would be the first to sympathize with the people of New Jersey).

"It's terrible to watch the agony of the young through all this. I feel so sad for them. If they can just hold out until they're forty." This was Celia's joke. Thirty was the age beyond which many students vowed they would not proceed.

"Well, they have their compensations. They seem to be freeing themselves from all our sexual hang-ups. I never saw anything on campus catch on so fast as this shacking-up. I guess two people try it and like it, and the word spreads." He smiled, and his fingers left the fringe to give her hair a friendly tug.

Celia laughed but was uneasy, and found herself lumbering for cover into serious discourse. "You don't worry that it's another foolhardy breach of the rules of living? What I'm thinking of is Rachel Carson's view of the organic whole that is the earth . . . the interrelationship of all the parts. Why eaglets are dying because the eggshells are too fragile from the DDT which comes from the mother eagles eating the fish from rivers fed by the run-off of farm fertilizer. It seems to me if people don't exercise *some* self-denial, it's the end of family, just as Lily Tucker says. Women will walk out. Why wouldn't they? I notice the same groups worried about eagles are awfully cavalier about the nesting places of human beings. In the next generation there'll be clean air and clean water and psychotic people."

Jacobs crossed his arms and stopped his teasing, and

Celia, finding herself too solemn, changed the subject again: "I meant to ask you. I have a good friend who's just returned for an advanced degree at your Institute. In psychology. Her name is Jessie Davidson. Do you know her?"

"She must be that older woman."

"She had the devil of a time getting you to take her."

"The point that's apt to be lost," he said sternly, "is that serious scholarship is like serious musicianship. To be an excellent pianist, you will have had to start playing by the age of five. And there is, God knows, enough dilettantish work being done already."

"Well, that's really an exclusionary point of view, isn't it? How handy for the men," said Celia, both indignant and amused. "You'd better not let Lily hear you say that if you want to woo her. Or for that matter, I don't like to hear it either. I'm thinking of becoming just that!" She gave a good scratch where all the hair had been tugged.

"Just what?" he asked, chastened. He was also reengaged by a flurried Celia, and by the words about wooing Lily.

"A dilettante. I think of spending my declining years a dilettante, a strict and fervently dedicated dilettante."

"Your declining years! It's too *soon*. You're at the top of your form!" The light coming through the rainy window dappled Celia, made an impressionist painting of a girl out of her.

"No doubt," said the old girl. "So it's a question of the inevitability of the descent. Outside there will be the vulgar racket of the last of civilization barreling over the cliff—Philip's certain Nixon is going to win—and inside, there I'll be, a sort of partial recluse, a celibate, holed up and reading its history and literature—till the flames reach me. I'm willing to do the light housework in exchange."

"What do you mean celibate? You don't want to skip the only boon in this benighted age! There's more to learning than history and literature! I speak with authority." He smiled.

"Yes, there are the languages. I don't know any languages. I don't know whether to start with Latin or Greek. I know you are laughing at me . . ."

"I won't."

"But I've given this a lot of thought . . . and I've come to the conclusion that my own well-being—I know that it is contrary to current opinion—but for *me*, it depends more on what I'm thinking about than who I am sleeping with, and so of course it makes me anxious to look to the contents of my mind."

"Well, one doesn't *have* to preclude the other." He tried another hair tug but halfheartedly.

"No, I can't manage. I find I get very distracted by lust, by men, that sort of thing. I don't think I could handle all the clandestine meetings, the . . . how do you say? *Infrastructure.* No," she said firmly, and she put her hand on his to arrest it. "No, I want to make the third third of my life the best third—the worst of times the best of times. I want to become . . . an educated person. I look around, and there are . . . almost none. One of our girls had to read *The Waste Land* for school and she couldn't understand it, so I read it, and I couldn't understand it."

"Oh, it's only the racket of your civilization barreling over a cliff, that's all. That Nixon is going to be president, you know, one of 'the low on whom assurance sits as a silk hat on a Bradford millionaire . . .' "

"Oh, I understand *that*. It's the allusions, the references, six languages including Sanskrit . . . I'll be forty-five.

There's the yawning chasm of my ignorance. And there's the yawning time to get through. Well, I want to make a joint solution, fill it all up with learning."

Jacobs thought about this and had some moral support for her. "You know, Eliot, Yeats, Frost, they all remark some place or other that they had thought there was a pool of knowledge shared by all educated people, and that they could depend upon it to be understood, and that they found there wasn't such a pool anymore."

"Well, that's what I want to make my mind, a restocked pool."

"I suppose you could go back to school like your friend whatsername . . ."

"No, that wouldn't suit me at all. I want to make this best third a Glorious Third," she said and thought that was funny.

"Like the Glorious Fourth?"

"That's right. And to be under somebody's instruction, to submit to the choice of *other* people . . . be obliged to *listen*, to obey, to perform for someone else . . . I've done that. That's what I've done through the first two thirds. No, I like the privateness, a private achievement. And it will keep me off the streets. And then, if by some miracle this country is restored, is regenerated—well, then, there I'll be, a national resource!"

Celia was certainly in earnest, and Jacobs was touched by her. He said rather tenderly, "I'll tell you something. When Proust at last retreats to his room, to his work, he does so because he wants to prove that his life has been worthy of being lived."

Celia found that amazing to consider. She sat silent. After a few moments she said, "Do you know, that's really very moving. It makes my eyes tear. I suppose I could start with French. And then—could I read Proust?"

"It's gripping."

"Gripping!"

She laughed and said, "Well, do you think I could do it, eventually, in French?" And she looked at him with a kind of yearning, inspired by God knows what, and he looked back at her with a kind of yearning, and said, "Of course, French is a *marvelous* language," and they came into each other's arms.

Seven

IN competition with the amorous activity currently being bragged about in Celia's world, interest in her front-seat kiss would have been hard to generate. But to give her her fair due, the conflict and turmoil into which she was thrown, however paltry her transgression might have seemed to friends, was not caused by narrow and literal moral confusion. She did not balk before simple infidelity. Among the binary systems that are used to separate the better sort from the worse, like the wheat and chaff system, or the sheep and goat, there's always been one that measures your superiority in art, music, literature, engineering, and so on, by the amount and variety of sexual experience you want and/or get. Adherents of this system were now running riot, intimidating God knows how many millions who secretly knew they were hopeless underachievers, and effecting a cultural revolution just about the opposite of the one getting effected in China. Among those feeling intimidated was Celia.

A proper examination of Celia's failure to measure up

would rest on several *facts* of a socially scientific nature, on top of the biological *suggestion* that her mind was not, at forty-five, as liable as it once had been to harrying sexual fantasies. An anthropological fact, for instance, was that she was born into a tightbuttoned, denying bourgeoisie, and that her sexual titillation was culturally determined therefrom, and rested, alas for her, on a brushwork of delicacy—on what was forbidden, unspoken, and unseen. She was psychologically out of joint. The current crusade to yank down all the curtains and hike up all the skirts left a fast-shrinking *terra incognita* for her sort of sexual imagination. Imperceptibly (but conveniently for her intention for a cerebral third third of life) she began to feel less easily rousable, more interested in history and literature, and were it not for the racket of the exploding, clamorous libidinous demand to deny everything but denial, Celia might have proceeded without complications.

Instead she was left to feel naked by being clothed, and in danger of losing caste in an Erewhonian world.

It was either in order to counter the threat of expulsion from this new paradise coming up, or out of a confused vanity, that Celia pursued her policy of looking as alluring as possible. She was sending out the wrong message. It should be noted on her behalf, however, that she spent her formative years resembling her father, a tentative pale copy, without the least warning that she was destined in her middle years to deepen in tone and plane and turn handsome like her handsome mother. So it was from beneath a fair brow that she began to contemplate a future of intellectual rigor and austerity. Too confident, she tempted the Fates. Jacobs was their instrument. When Celia allowed him to understand that her vulnerability to passion was so remarkable that it must be strenuously avoided, she had given herself one air too many. After the kiss on Saturday night she went home and couldn't sleep, and the next morning she got up and couldn't think. Fortunately Sunday is a day for testifying, not thinking.

The Bronx is a large borough with a low, flat plain that spreads to the east for miles and finally reaches the Sound. Large sections of this plain were already well-blighted by urban decay and urban renewal, but there remained neighborhoods, many ranging acres wide, with block upon block of two-story houses, cheek by jowl, squat or slim, trees at the curb, and stucco stoops that on this Sunday morning were banked by a zillion azalea bushes blooming in an amazing intensity of oranges, fuchsias, reds. Major arteries cut through from west to east, but you might spend your whole life in the Bronx without ever turning off them, without ever registering the existence of these discrete, trim worlds—which Celia very nearly did. It was Marian who put her in the way of the broadening experience.

Although Marian lived way down at Washington Square, she located, or rather divined, what she believed to be an inspired site for a peace vigil, in what was in fact the land of her forefathers. She told Celia that she remembered as a very small child first a subway ride, then a trolley, then getting out by the Chateau de Luxe Ballroom, passing the fire station, crossing the cobblestones, not turning her ankle, and finally, a grandmother in an apron holding up two floury hands. Now, half a century later, she had strung out her vigil on a bridge built over an artery to connect the old neighborhoods, and the bonus for her purposes was that on either side of the bridge was a church. The very popular

Sts. Cosmas and Damien in red brick and the locally admired stucco was on the one side, and the less well-attended
dark-shingled Presbyterian church on the other.

As Washington Square was, so the East Bronx was not,
demographically speaking, saturated with potential vigilers,
and this was certainly because of the soldier-sons of the
indigenes, who wanted them to win. Every Sunday they
drove across the bridge past the vigil, live and let live, and
prayed for the annihilation of the enemy. Meanwhile Marian
had inspired unbelievable loyalty from a small legion of
non-church and non-synagogue-going moralists from the
non-Bronx. Weekly they straggled up and strung themselves across the bridge, church to church, and many of
them no doubt stood immobilized by the weight of their
misgivings at lending themselves to this fruitless observance.
It was out of fealty to Marian, who was not grateful, that
Celia regularly turned up, but in a kind of compensation
talked through the whole hour of silence with a friend she
had made on the line. This was her bridge friend, Jessie
Davidson.

That morning had begun with a new spring sun, and the
wet lawns around the castle were beginning to steam and
smell of earth, but Celia could not wait to stand in the
miasma of the bridge, which was cross-ventilated by ex-
haust fumes from the artery below and the church traffic
stalled in front. Jessie had gotten there first, looking from a
distance like a boy, small-boned, graceful, a Roman gladiator with a dark, tight-curled perfect head. Close at hand she
seemed more nearly her forty years, and more literally a
gladiator (from Georgia instead of Rome) if by gladiator is
meant one who fights in public for the amusement of the

people. Jessie had five children too. She explained to Celia that this was a cultural rather than personal coincidence since their appointed time to marry fell after the defeat of Hitler when educated women expressed a humanist solidarity with all victims by democratically giving birth as mindlessly as they could manage. She said this was typical of what they had taken lying down.

Jessie also lived at Washington Square and in fact shared an elevator shaft with Marian, waiting before which they had become friends. She was married to the surgeon of Celia's parable and had until recently and with meticulous attention supervised the intricate comings and goings of each member of her family, which she called her patient load. Generally speaking, Jessie subscribed to a conspiratorial view of everything and tried to teach Celia to see things in her light. She had long since considered the feasibility of leaving her husband for reasons, she said encouragingly, that might equally apply for Celia. Also, she had had an affair. "He did not take me unawares. I deliberately set out. I would not want to die with a record of rectitude like yours, Celia," she said, in a voice that still retained traces of the gentle South, and she added, "My Lord, it's no big deal." Meanwhile she had also laid siege to the Institute of Graduate Studies. After two years it yielded, and inside she found they were no big deal either.

On the retailing of the newest advances in permissivism, Jessie was certainly Celia's chief supplier. Although on the value of sexual freedom Jessie the Citizen was latitudinarian, Jessie the Mother got very eclectic when it came to her own teenage children.

"Oh," sighed Celia, who sounded like Flossie, the Bobbsey

twin, when talking to Jessie. "It's so hard to be young today with everybody caving in. I mean we grew up in a world where there were rules of behavior and we behaved them."

"*You* behaved them," Jessie said. Celia's innocence, her uninformed condition, strained Jessie's belief, and she felt alternately that she had been sent to toughen her, and to protect her. "There is only one of you left. There are forty-six whooping cranes."

Going to the vigil had come to feel for Celia like sneaking off the preserve. She took her place as the straight man, her clear brow, her everyday fine-grained integrity weighing in very little. But on this particular Sunday she was in a breathless fret to ask a casual, offhand question of Jessie. Did she happen to know K. P. Jacobs? At the Institute?

"Everybody knows who he is," said Jessie.

"What's he like?"

"Herzog."

"Herzog?"

"Didn't you ever read *Herzog?*"

"Well, I suppose you mean he's the sort of sensitive Jewish intellectual who's been . . . driven to despair by everything coming together . . . corrupt society . . . childhood guilt . . ." Celia said, a little defensive, scurrying to establish her own intellectual sensitivity.

"I mean he's the kind of real fine fellow with a colossal ego, spends all his time wearing out the world's beautiful women, never can get satisfied, nobody *quite* good enough. Too bad. Out you go. Move along. Till one fine day he gets to be forty and lo and behold all of a sudden he can't keep the pace. He's got himself married to a woman he can't service. *She's* not satisfied. Out *she* goes! That's the time when he gets crushed by the corrupt society. I don't actually know him."

"I don't think you have to worry about libel laws up here."

"I only mean, if you are thinking of taking him on, he's a ranked player. Probably do you a world of good. Get you out of that house."

Jessie talked joyously on. She did not confine herself to Jacobs but went through the other senior scholars in the Institute, raunchy fellows notwithstanding their advanced average age. Celia listened and laughed and was increasingly excited by the forbidden vulgarity of Jacobs' reputation, as ruined by Jessie. The temptation of a virtuous woman to depart from her model behavior *on principle* is an overlooked phenomenon. Were Celia to join Jacobs' list of conquests it might be for her after all like losing one's anonymity by being a woman Frank Harris loved. Recollection of the actual Jacobs disturbed this idyll. Celia said, "You're going to be just stunned if you ever meet him, Jessie. He looks like such a quiet, scholarly . . ."

"They all look like that!"

"Marian and Tennie have known him for years. They seem to think that he's . . . *forlorn* and in need of a companion. In fact Tennie and Philip have found a really dazzling young . . ." Celia proceeded with an outline of their cupid-playing.

"Sounds to me like Susannah and the Elders," said Jessie.

"Well, I just think you are assassinating the wrong character."

When the hour was up, Marian loped down the line to confront them. She had not actually ever rebuked Celia and

Jessie for their animating an otherwise sober-faced row of mourners, since she was above all interested in a body count, but she certainly never thought them worthy of carrying a sign. Marian was one of those fortunate people who attempt to bury pain in angry activity and succeed. Her handsome face with wide cheekbones was getting weathered with all the marching.

"I just want to know whether you are or you aren't going to be in France on Friday?" she said to Celia impatiently, no hello. Her supply of impatience had become inexhaustible. Celia stalled.

"France? My Lord, when you going to France?" Jessie asked, surprised.

"Because I'm going to have to have a light supper for Peter after the talk on Sunday. Just a few of us. I don't want to get into anything elaborate," Marian pursued.

"You didn't tell me you were going to France!" Jessie said accusingly.

"I forgot," said Celia, who had forgotten she was going to France.

"Friday! You mean you don't even know whether you're going to France on Friday? Well, now I call that very cool. So," said Jessie with a half-lidded look into the distance, "I'm putting two and two together . . ."

"I suppose you know K. P. Jacobs?" Marian asked Jessie.

"Only by reputation," Jessie said with reserve.

"Well, if you and Eph want to come over to dinner on Sunday you'll have to go to the lecture first," said Marian briskly. "Let me know tonight. I've got a hundred things on this week. But I certainly think he's worth a meal. He's one of the few people Tennie publishes who's really a first-rate mind—sound, scholarly."

Celia, all at once inspired, offered to relieve Marian and take on the supper. She said Philip was overworked and showing the strain, and it would be a shorter evening for him. Marian said, "When are you going to stop being a handmaiden to that man?"—her way of accepting the kind offer.

Jessie said, "I certainly think she should start applying to graduate schools. Maybe you can work a deal with this fellow Jacobs. I look forward to meeting him, I'm sure!"

"I told her she was a fool not to go back to school," said Marian. "Didn't I say you were a fool?"

"Oh, yes, she did," said Celia bobbing her head emphatically to Jessie.

Eight

By midafternoon of the next day, Monday, Miss Callahan, Philip's secretary, had sent up by messenger Celia's ticket to Paris and Marseilles for the coming Friday. Swift were the way things were done at *The State*. That evening neither Philip, who did not want to queer his plans by over-attention, nor Celia, who did not intend to fly on Friday, mentioned the ticket. How it was that she found herself unable to say casually, "Oh, say, listen, I've put off my trip until the 6th—I just need the extra few days," she did not know. In part it was because Philip would surely have argued, and she would have had to defend her decision, as he always did and she never could. And did Philip's sudden solicitude for the welfare of his enemy her mother cause Celia to wonder about his purposes? She did not wonder for a moment about his purposes.

He worried about his own purposes. People who thought Philip austere in his composure would have been surprised to hear that he was emotionally susceptible as they found themselves, and that currently, while appearing particularly wearily cool, he was intensely absorbed by not one, but two, passions. He did not in fact *love* Lily. But he loved Hubert Humphrey. Twenty years ago at the Democratic Convention in Philadelphia Humphrey established his integrity forever with Philip. Now, for Philip, this was not a lost leader, but a man fallen on evil times. He was sure Humphrey, if elected, would end the war, as he was sure Nixon wouldn't. And he was sure the continued fratricidal battle among the Democrats would defeat them all. One did not have to be a particularly astute political analyst to see things this way. All one had to do was get up in the morning. Nonetheless, it was not for these reasons that Philip was going to support Humphrey, it was for the love long since lodged in him. Twenty years ago Celia had not had the affecting experience at the Democratic Convention, and the above reasons did not answer her sense of betrayal.

Now Humphrey had announced formally that he had joined the race. The timing, for Philip's purposes, was suddenly excellent. He scheduled *The State's* editorial support for the issue coming out on the 6th, with Lily's offensive review, balling everything up in one shot, with Celia off and away. They were making up the cover now. It was a company secret.

The secret leaked.

On Tuesday morning, beset by a lonely-at-the-top gloom, he strode through the reception room in silence and went into his office to take a call.

"Well, old boy, I hear you're going to be the first on board," said Tennie, in his casual drawl. There was no doubt about on board what.

"Jesus, Tennie, I just want to get it over with. What do you think?" Philip said, sorry the second he asked.

"I think it won't make a damn bit of difference to any-body with the exception of Marian and by marriage me. She has the notion I wield an influence over you, you know—for the worse, usually."

"And *Celia*," Philip added, in case Tennie thought the world was short of martyrs.

"Celia, yes. She's certainly going to be very upset," Tennie concurred cheerfully.

"Well, look here, Tennie, I'd appreciate it if you didn't say anything. She takes off on Friday before it's out, and by the time she gets back I'm hoping that the whole thing will have subsided somewhat."

"She's not going *Friday*."

"Yes, *Friday*."

"Well, Marian says she's giving the dinner after the Jacobs lecture on *Sunday*. I can't understand why you don't know when she's going. Don't you two talk to each other?"

"For God's sake! Sunday! That's the Lord's Day! And why the hell are we going to Jacobs' lecture? 'Vico and Yeats's Gyres,' what the hell is all that about? Don't tell me! I don't want to know. Listen, he's been giving this series for the last ten years without my hearing him. I believe I can make it through the next ten!" Philip rattled all this into the phone to scatter Tennie and give himself time to think.

"It was Lily's idea. You don't have to go. He's a Heavens-gate author so I do." Tennie always sounded unruffled, half-amused, but he was subject to worse headaches than Philip was, which Philip knew.

"It's this damn Columbia business. I've been racing around, went over to scout it out myself last night. It's a bad scene, as they say. I haven't had time for two words with my own wife," embroidered the beleaguered editor to his brother.

That evening, to his own wife who had botched his brainstorm of a plan, he grumbled, "So, you've put off your trip?"

"Not *far* off. Just until Monday. There are so many loose ends, you know . . ."

"What about your mother? Does she—"

"Well, I had written to her, and then I tried to get through to her today, but the Côte de Rhône phone operators are working to rule, and there's a slowdown . . ."

"Maybe it would be better after all if you made the Friday flight," Philip's voice warbled winningly.

"I thought if I couldn't reach her tomorrow, you wouldn't mind going through channels. Maybe Miss Callahan . . ." Celia's mind was fixed on its own intentions.

"She had the devil of a time getting you a seat on that Friday flight. What in heaven's name made you change your mind?" He thought he was entitled to be irritable.

"Change my mind? I didn't change my mind. I hadn't made it up. You made it up," said Celia pointedly. "There are just a lot of little things—Harriet's SATs are on Saturday, and you know, Marian's quite put out about my not showing up for the march, so I thought I could make it up to her by our having supper *here* after Peter's lecture, instead of there. I knew she'd rather, and I knew you'd rather."

Ordinarily this would have soothed Philip. He believed Marian was not only a bad cook but had a bad cook. Moreover, increasingly these last years he liked to have dinner in his own house. Then when it was time to go home, he was.

"And I don't want to worry you," said Celia, "but I am

uneasy about Francie, with this Columbia trouble I wanted to wait the weekend out. She says she's broken off with Forster, but . . . and she and Nell are so politically wrought up . . ."

Celia had aimed at the vulnerability of the father, but she could not know how exposed he felt. He sat back in his chair with a poof and a grunt, and put his hand on the phone for comfort. His was a large wing chair from which he also had control over the music on FM. Celia's was middle-sized and controlled the knitting basket. Philip turned on the radio, dependable Mozart, picked up the *Post*, and thought, those girls are certainly going to be hurt and angry when they see the Humphrey endorsement. They'll think I didn't listen. But he had listened to his girls intently from the first word of the first child, strained to hear every question. Correspondingly, he had long practice in fielding fine answers. They were God knows a very verbal family, and he superintended their development down to their very verbs. They could not say "communicate" even though he was in the communications business.

Now Bess came in. She was fourteen and had not yet begun to get long and thin, to her grief. She backed onto her father, and looking from one parent to the other, began to talk in a serious, careful way, as somebody might report spotting a new species to fellow bird-watchers. "Something very interesting happened to me today in math. I always thought that when people weren't nice, when they were mean, you know? Well, that they were just ordinary people but they were *acting* nasty. Well, then, all of a sudden I got this terrific . . ." She groped for her word.

"Insight?" suggested Celia.

"*Insight*, that's right. Suddenly I saw that some people

didn't just behave nasty. They *were* nasty! They were *nasty people.*" And she added quietly, "I already have quite a list."

Polly had been dancing at the door impatiently, with needles and wool of her own. "It's the commercial, mama. I did something wrong. You've got to hurry."

Celia took up the knitting and said, "Well, *Bess* wouldn't be on anybody's list."

"She's been on mine," said Polly.

Philip shooed them off. He thought it was really phenomenal with so many claims on him, mind and heart, that he could find a minute for a lusting thought, let alone plans for a consummation. It took a man of mettle.

Nine

In the history of the Decline of the West the exact year that it fell off the top of the bell curve was either 1968 or 1970. Experts may never agree. In the week before Celia's departure, Philip personally thought he felt the whole thing go over. That week, the events, item by item, that crossed his desk were cumulatively of such appalling moral gravity as to leach down through his defenses and depress him badly. (The Czechoslovakian Spring was the only bright spot.) In particular the microcosm of Columbia was to Philip a revolution, unlike the good old revolutions, with no heroes, nothing fine. What should have been boys and girls were rutting animals, shrieking, obscene. Twice he called Francie at Smith, and twice she was at the other end, gloomily reassuring her father that Columbia was the last thing she cared about. Gloomily her father warned, "Monday we come out for Humphrey, baby." "Columbia is the next to the last thing," was her only comment.

The amount of suffering the middle classes do is terribly disproportionate to their share in the world's distribution of things. It cannot be justified. At critical moments in this particular spring the American educated liberal, a spin-off of these classes, was in a chaos of painful division, one large group twisting against itself, finding its own philosophy worse than bankrupt, finding liberalism to blame for the bombing of peasants. Philip did not belong to this group. Neither as a liberal in regard to the war, nor as a white in regard to slavery did he find himself ultimately culpable. Self-castigation was not his style. Instead, and much more reasonably, and item by item through the week, Philip grew very angry at his wife.

The annoyance began quite naturally with her postponement of his plans for her, and it increased by leaps with her bouncy and undeflectable intention to forward his project for joining Jacobs and Lily, since he didn't have this project anymore. And when the Yeats lecture was cancelled because of general strife in university circles, she might have redeemed herself by calling off the supper, but she said she had already stuffed the cannelloni.

Then in the middle of this week he got an altogether unexpected and gratuitous jolt. Philip had what is called a comfortable income, but fixed. He was generous to Celia with their money and had put $5,000 at her disposal in a special joint account, but it was rarely touched, so good a provider was he. On Thursday after supper, strolling past the bankbook drawer in Celia's desk, he mechanically, as he did from time to time, took a look at the balance, which he should not have done in a week there was no evidence God was in his heaven. There was scarcely any balance. On the stubs were noted $750 for Eugene McCarthy, $250 for Robert Kennedy (he understood Celia's moral arithmetic), and a third, splutter, splutter, was $4,000 to Mary-Louise

Catchpole. It took Philip some time to collect himself. He went downstairs and found Celia washing dishes and said, "Listen Sweetheart"—when Philip was angry he called her Listen Sweetheart the way Humphrey Bogart did when he was angry—"Listen, sweetheart, I was just innocently going through your desk drawer, and without any warning I discover that you've given away five thou."

"Oh," said Celia, with an apologetic tilt of her head to the sink. "Yes, I forgot. I wanted to talk to you about it."

"It's a damn funny little item to forget," he said, unbelieving.

"The trip just wiped it out of my mind," she lied.

"You know it scares the hell out of me when I think there's a leaky sieve somewhere."

"For years you've assured me, Philip, that that money was there for me in case I wanted it. You said you always wanted me to feel free about . . ."

"I certainly didn't think you were going to feel free about supporting the Catchpoles with it."

"Well, I didn't feel free."

"I can't imagine what the hell they're . . . I certainly think you should at least have talked it over with me. I certainly . . ."

This exchange continued in a constrained tone for a while. During it each alternately acknowledged feeling surprise and pain owing to the attitude of the other. At the end of the matter, Philip was at least satisfied that Catchpole himself wouldn't have gotten the money, but Celia still had the surprise and pain.

Meanwhile Philip could not get a line through to Agnes, increasing his resentment against a woman whose mother's phone company had such poor labor relations. And when he finally, on Friday, and with reluctance, called UPI in Paris on this personal matter, it was to hear from a voice quite hysterical with joy that yesterday's "student unrest" in Paris had turned into revolutionary violence. They were tearing up the streets.

It was the last straw. It brought Philip back full circle to home base. They must close ranks. And he threw Celia into the breach. Celia, who might have been on her way to France by now, must be stopped altogether. Lily was thrust out from the center to the dim edge of his consciousness. With a sense of great personal sacrifice he forgot to think about her.

He called Celia, described the Left Bank situation, and told her to cancel her flight. She said, "Don't be silly." She, who had protested, delayed, dragged her heels, and lost her passport, was now in a fever to be off.

He said, "You don't seem to understand. There's some danger. People are getting hurt."

"Oh, for goodness sake, Philip. I'm only changing planes there." All of a sudden she was intrepid, in full sail, in reverse.

He said, "Air terminals are the obvious first targets for terrorists."

"The air terminals will be filled with peace delegates. I'm quite sure they won't want to blow up peace delegates."

As is usual about crises in flux, everybody has an ardent opinion, people who are uninformed, people who are misinformed: the whole gamut. Celia added in her stern tone used to correct children, "What is the matter with you, dear? You are usually the one to take the least alarm."

Philip called Tennie. Philip liked hearing things first and telling Tennie. This suited the needs of Tennie who, as lord of his own domain, had one eyebrow always raised in part to signify that whatever it was, he already knew.

"Listen, I just spoke to UPI in Paris. They've closed the Sorbonne. They're cutting down trees and digging up paving stones on the Boul' Mich. They've strung up barricades. They're linking up with the unions. Those kids really know how to run a revolution," Philip said, meaning to asperse our kids.

" 'They order this matter better in France,' " said Tennie, quoting from *A Sentimental Journey,* confident that Philip wouldn't recognize it.

"My God, they certainly do! They're a damn sight closer to a student-worker alliance than these damn fools with their Harlem uprising." The Columbia students had hoped to be joined by their neighbors in the ghetto. They were still hoping.

"They don't make proletarians with real mind and heart anymore," Tennie said. He was of course a liberal too. He belonged to that subspecies for whom the year 1910 was the West's watershed, and he used the same casual mocking style to cover a reverence for ideas that were thought before that date, and to express a contempt for those after. Tennie would be the last one to accuse himself of starting the war in Southeast Asia.

"Celia's hell-bent on going off Monday anyhow," said Philip. "Maybe I just ought to put my foot down and tell her she can't go."

"That'll be interesting," said Tennie in his flat way.

Philip let a moment slip and then said, strained, "Well, I guess we see you Sunday," instead of good-by.

"We bring the cheesecake," said Tennie, instead of good-by.

"You mean Lily?"

"I *mean* from Sutters. Lily's a big girl. She can get up there under her own steam."

Philip put down the phone surprised for the moment to learn that Lily seemed also to have been discarded by his brother. At first his alarm increased with the thought the ship must really be about to founder if even Tennie was into lightening his cargo, but he knew that Tennie believed that the ship had already gone down. The measure of Philip's anguish was that he did not wonder more about this. And Sunday evening Lily would not in fact turn up under her own steam. She would be escorted by Peter Jacobs. Lily was a buoyant little skiff, all right.

It was not clear whether Lily knew how many elders had been engaged in making plans for her future, or what plans. They put her into a fickle position. Whether she was herself fickle, was another question; the answer was, somewhat. She insincerely wavered in her feeling of attraction for the two courtly, finely tailored brothers with their money and power, who were standing on their heads to make themselves intriguing.

In the round of phoning that was done over the cancelled lecture and the proceeding supper, Celia, her major problem still unresolved, confided to Lily that she did not know what books to take with her to France. Lily said *The Second Sex*. She herself, Lily said, was very interested in de Beauvoir's idea that human relationships are to be perpetually invented, that *a priori* no form is privileged, none impossible. Celia said, "What do you mean?" "Oh, only that the idea that marriage has some sort of prescriptive entitlement is a fiction, that's all." Celia said she thought that living meant choosing from among the wealth of cultural

fictions, and would Lily feel it was a good idea or a discarded fictional form to have Peter Jacobs swing round to
get her and bring her to the supper? Lily thought it had
antique charm.

Marian, for whom Lily was a passing thought, dismissed
her for playing the ingénue to two aging fools. Marian was
one of those people who are tenderhearted about their own
younger selves, and taken an Edenic view of childhood
generally, believing parents are the serpent. She was a fore-
runner among those who discovered how repressive it was
to make children be tidy and polite. This ought currently
to have been an immense advantage for hers. Children will
not obey any theory about them, Marian's included, but regardless of what they became, she continued to see the
young, specifically the male young, through sentimental
eyes. Her draft-evading counsel brought her in daily con-
tact with them, a satisfaction compounded, which is not to
cast doubt on her integrity. But the notion that either
Tennie or Philip would prove himself the object of a young
girl's passionate desire was beyond her imagination. That a
middle-aged woman might want a young man was understandable to her, but a young woman vice versa really
wasn't.

It was to Celia. It was easy for Celia to credit the attraction an older man had for a young girl. She had been that
sort of young girl herself, whether the consequence of a
simple psychological mechanism frequently discovered to
be operating in daughters with adored fathers, or for un-
fathomable reasons. And Celia could with impunity put
Lily in the way of Peter not even knowing if Lily had the
requisite adored father or not. She did this. She had drawn
back from that front-seat kiss and said, "I'm not able to

cope with this, Peter, and I mean it. I commend you to Lily," and laughed, and Peter had moved back to his side of the car with just barely enough reluctance to offer her a second go, and they went on to talk into the night. And that was not the end of that for anybody.

It is true that Celia could not sleep or remember she was going to France, and that when this journey was forced on her attention by the delivery of her ticket, she allowed herself to stall long enough to attend the next appointed rendezvous with Peter, a public one, the lecture. But it was not true that she was a heroine wrestling with the same scruples as heroines of yore, quite apart from her being twice the age of females in whom in the old days passions raged. But for her, as well as for Philip (and of course many other people), it was a time of terrible vulgar discredit, when all institutions, philosophies, principalities were in the hands of the public relations industry. If Celia faltered before the choice of good and bad, it was because it seemed the forces of good had tipped against self-denial.

It is in the romantic tradition that to be good is to give up what one craves. Self-denial had previously been the heart and soul of virtue. George Eliot's little Tina was tortured by loving above her station. A scoundrel had trifled with her. He would have to be a scoundrel because Tina was good, and would not have fallen in love with a fine handsome, intelligent fellow from an upper class. There might have been a dozen possible opinions about how to resolve her predicament, but all would involve denial. None would have been, "Go on, you owe it to yourself. You not only have a right but a duty to have gratifying sexual relations, little Tina. To deny physical satisfaction to your awakened passion is mentally unhealthy and also hypocritical, and also marks you as somebody liable to intimidation by the establishment, the very establishment which has just fought against the American colonists' right to their liberty, and which, in the event that a revolution breaks out in, say, France [this was 1788], would be against the oppressed people. Are you really a free spirit?" The case for infidelity could be very moving.

And the case against had loopholes. Celia did not believe with Lily and Simone de Beauvoir that among the forms of relationships marriage wasn't privileged, in spite of the acknowledged fact that the American family was the breeding ground of the people in the Pentagon. A European regard for family was closer to what she held, although the Europeans were abandoning it. That is to say, Celia thought of family as having corporate claims of overriding worth. She thought that if possible a borderline marriage should not be broken or dismantled, but ducked out of, for relief, and in this she was very close to the cultural assumptions embedded in the heads of the mothers of the heroines of yore, the aforementioned Mrs. Bennets, Primroses, Lathams. So that philosophically she would have been able to subscribe to her own infidelity were she to have been suffering with Philip.

But suffering was changing. The threshold for it had dropped dramatically in the great egalitarian putsch, opening vistas of vulnerability never dreamed of. Celia was not immune to the assault of new suggestions about what constituted deprivation, what was intolerable.

Jessie said, "What I want is for all my *big* mistakes to be behind me. When you're young it is appropriate to make wrong choices. But at forty for a woman worth anything it's her nick of time. She's twice as much person as when she was twenty. She learns more selectively. She loves more appreciatively. And meanwhile opportunities abound. You've got to be in charge of your own experience, Celia. There are six billion people in the world. You going to get to the end of a long life and look back and say you only slept with one of them?"

"Oh, for heaven's sake, Jessie. I'd just give my eye teeth to be roused by a man's *mind*," Celia said, a watery answer.

"Gracious me, I think you quite sincerely believe that," Jessie said, unrebuffed.

Peter Jacobs had also roused Celia's *mind*. One good reason is that he seemed really interested in what she had on it. The disparity with Philip was very wide here.

"Tennie told me a wonderful thing about Ruskin," said Celia at dinner one evening in the middle of this parlous week. "Ruskin was very fervent against the use of iron in architecture. Do you want to know why?"

Philip looked semiconscious.

The children asked why, but their mother was wanting an adult response, and she faltered before pressing on. "Well, I guess he didn't like iron. But," she said, talking to Philip through the children, "he was able to fit whatever he didn't like into the grand scheme of things. He could make it be morally wrong. In the case of cast iron, he said that architecture was the first art and God . . ."

"What do you mean, first art?" asked Polly.

"People want to have houses before they want pictures to hang in them, do you see?" (She saw.) "And Ruskin said that God left stone and wood and clay lying about for the first primitive people to get on with it, to build their houses, but He didn't have iron lying about. He *could* have but He didn't, because He knew, according to Ruskin, that it wasn't really good-looking. Well, what I mean is," she said, turning from the children to Philip, "what a luxury to live in a time when you could be so *sure* of divine purpose."

"Nobody reads Ruskin anymore," said Philip, with inexplicable bad temper. "Tennie's wasting his time and money."

"First you have to believe God put the stone and wood and clay there," Celia said firmly. "Then you have to believe that *you* caught on to His purpose. Actually I think it represents an immense and quite ingenuous confidence in one's own perception. Nobody can have confidence like that anymore. *Nobody,*" Celia added, with a short, mean look at Philip.

"I'm really very glad you told us about Ruskin, mother," said Bess enthusiastically. "I never have heard of him before." She was a child who did not like any divisions between two parents.

"I'd really like to see an iron house," said Polly, another child who didn't. In fact the three girls expressed two minutes' worth of great interest in Ruskin.

Nothing to compare with Peter's. Celia had told him about Ruskin that night of the car, and he was really intrigued. "Is that so? Isn't that interesting? Let's see, that would be about . . . when? Well, just about when Darwin . . . say 1860. It's a nice bit, fits in very well. I'm always looking for a new metaphor, something fresh. By the time, you see, you get to the end of the century, Yeats—or Joyce for that matter—they're sort of casting about for something to replace the Christian cosmology. And of course that's how they discover Vico . . ."

Celia could not hear enough about Vico.

Ten

O<small>N</small> the castle half-acre, as far as the early blooming of the lilacs, the two pink cherry trees, the early leafing of the pin oaks and the copper beeches, were auspices of coming world events they were bad, in that they would not prove to have been a good omen of anything later discernible. Pity the world. But as prognostications for Celia's supper, they were fair in their promise. The party was a happy comedy. Any number of guests might have made the tedious trip to the Duponts muttering, and returned home in the belief that the time spent there had been prosperous, pleasant and desirable. Dante called his work *The Divine Comedy* not because of the ghastly irony of things, but because the conclusion was prosperous, pleasant and desirable. Several guests were cheered right from the moment they heard they would not have to listen to the Yeats lecture.

At the party there were a lot of people, a lot of cannelloni, a lot of (union) lettuce, and two ten-dollar cheesecakes besides the priceless Lily. There were in fact thirty-odd people because Heavensgate and Peter combined had obligations that Marian readily transferred to Celia—and it may not be too awry to mention here that since Marian did believe that Celia and Philip *inter alia* were responsible for the Vietnam War, she thought no efforts at restitution were too much to ask (and none enough). For Celia, the blessed omen of the lovely summery day meant a party that could spill out on the porch for a while, a much less starchy affair, menu apart.

Five of the thirty at supper were the daughters of the house. They would eat the most. Francie and Nell had come home for the weekend, although it was the middle of exam period, to wish their mother farewell: ostensibly. Fare well: Francie took the opportunity to weep, to express her unrelenting misery, disgust, sense of betrayal, permanent disillusionment, until her murmuring mother, who had strains of her own, bellowed, "For God's sake, I can't stand it anymore! You've got to learn to take *comfort*, to be *appeasable*. Nobody is awarded the luxury of such *endless* self-concern. Every one of you children thinks you have the right to bring every bit of personal pain to me and destroy my peace for the entire day!" To which Francie responded severely, "*You* wanted to be the mother!" and went loftily off.

Meanwhile, suspecting the woolly mammoth lurking, the father promised to take both girls to the Met game Sunday where he had seats in the press box. They did not care about baseball, but they would go because they were crazy about their father. Nell cared about music and poetry and was the only living American known to have stayed up all night because she could not put down *The Faerie Queen*. Also, she was the one child who was small and dark, taking after old Mother Dupont, and the peacemaker in a family of sometimes furious doves. Francie had come down to the party in a dress (required) and hiking boots, and it was Bess who talked her around to sandals to spare a row. Both girls fell under the spell of Lily.

Lily did not like Yeats, something the matchmakers had not taken into account.

Lily and Peter had arrived early in full argument about Yeats's metaphysical beliefs. Celia saw they annoyed each other and was pleased, Philip delighted.

". . . his fixation with Vico, and the plotting of all that elaborate astrological nonsense!" Lily was overflowing.

"*Exactly*," said Philip.

"Some of his poetry is of course *first-rate*, and *relevant*," Lily continued. " 'Did that play of mine send out/ Certain men the English shot?' *More* than relevant."

The eyes of the four daughters present, Francie, Nell, Harriet, and Bess, slid for a moment toward their father's face to see how he took that forbidden word "relevant." He took it fine. Philip was in fact overjoyed by Lily's evident dismissal of both Peter and Vico. He himself had no sooner heard of Vico than he was sick of him. Celia had just this week asked what he knew about him, a name never even mentioned in City College, certainly never mentioned at Yale Law.

Nell, the poetry lover, said shyly, "I think Yeats must have suffered so much from his unrequited love for Maud Gonne."

"Oh!" said Lily. "Poor, long-suffering *woman*. Just to be pursued like that, *interminably*. She was absolutely right! And what's the most outrageous is that she worked her *whole life* for Irish independence, she was an active *feminist,* an intellectually astute person in *every way,* and the only thing anybody knows about her is that she wouldn't sleep with Yeats! Some memorialist! Well, I admire her tremendously. I have tremendous *empathy* with her."

Another forbidden word, and still the father couldn't have seemed more contented. Jacobs, on the other hand, shifted about, and said, "An argument could be made, you know, that the idea of empathy was born with Vico, or at least . . ."

Celia longed to hear that argument.

". . . and she was one of the first to see that men were inherently too *egotistical,* too conceited to let their wives develop fully," Lily went on, not ready to be sidetracked. "If a married woman really has something worthwhile *to do* in the world, she thought, her husband will *stop* her . . .

Throughout the evening it was Lily's voice and Lily's theme, although what she said would not have been all that heady in an ordinary exchange between two people. But everybody selected a pointed message to be the eye-opener for somebody else. The female members of the extended Dupont family were all pleased that the males were attending. Of the male members, one was delighted to attend, and one wasn't. Even Marian took mildly approving notice of Lily this evening. In the first place, the impassioned declamation was Marian's preferred form of discourse, and in the second she knew that Lily had approached Tennie for a change in her status and had been turned back, and Marian as well as the next was generous with the failed as long as they stayed failed. She attributed Lily's ebullience to her defeat.

However, they had put three arrows in Lily's quiver, and since the first one fell to earth she knew not where, she sent the next one toward Philip with no loss of momentum. When she finished saying, "Yeats is not where the action is," she turned and said pointedly to Tennie who had just ambled by, "and God knows Ruskin isn't. I suppose I must sound like a Yahoo . . .

"Yes, you do," said Tennie.

"Well, in fact I would like to remind you that I supported the Ruskin project when it came up. But you've got Janus for a colophon. You're only committed to looking backwards *half* the time. And I offered to help you break into the future—but you turned me down," she finished good-naturedly, as if not getting what one wanted was as good a joke as getting it. Tennie kept a stone face. Philip's pulses beat happily.

Lily provided the major focus for *almost* everybody. Peter found a place next to Celia and said, "I haven't been able to get you out of my mind."

Celia flushed.

"I find myself staring at the shelves in my office . . . scanning them to see what books might be right for you."

Celia had misflushed.

"The more I think about your proposal, the more exciting it seems to me it can be. I hope you won't mind but I've taken the liberty . . ."

Jessie Davidson and Tennie joined them. Jessie had been taking Jacobs's measure all evening, and now in a mild but authentic drawl she said, "I'm right anxious to know, Professor Jacobs, where I might read some of your Vico on the off chance I have an hour to kill." She laughed boldly. He laughed warily.

"Well," he said, "do you know *To the Finland Station?*"

"I take it that's not a timetable for the railroads?"

"And of course, better still, Cornell University Press is coming out with the first English translation of *Scienza Nuova.*"

"My God, what a first!" said Philip, who was passing through. "Eat your heart out, Tennie, you missed another winner," and he was off.

Celia looked stern. Jessie said to Tennie, "Talk about first, I hear your brother's going to be the first sonafabitch to come out for Humphrey."

Tennie turned to Celia and said, "Well, you can't say I was the one who told you," looked especially bored, and left.

Jessie, made remorseful by the tightened expression on Celia's face, said, "My Lord, Celia, there can't be a person here tonight blames you for this."

And then Peter said very gracefully, and yet very sternly, "There's no point in making a pariah out of Philip. He's just holding the center for us, if I may use a worn . . ." and with an eye to two of Celia's daughters who were listening with stiff expressions, he proceeded to dilate upon the essentially heroic nature of their father's act, of what others might loosely but wrongly call trimming.

Celia had certainly known the endorsement was in the works, but was stricken by how quickly Philip had acted, and her immediate, understandable reaction was indignation that he hadn't the courage to tell her first. Women of a gentle and soft-spoken manner do not see themselves as ever being dreadable. Now as Celia listened to Peter's dignified defense of Philip and watched her girls, visibly relieved, able to take comfort, she found herself delivered with unexpected ease from a stretch of bitter domestic tension she had thought inevitable. Here in a moment, Peter had brought her through the personal ordeal of it on a breeze. He could read her gratitude in her confusion.

Before the party was over, Peter sought her out again in private and said, "I wanted to tell you, I have something for you. I hope you'll be pleased, and that you won't mind my . . . you won't think that I am intruding?"

"Of *course* not."

"You talk about where to start, not wanting to scatter too *thinly*, and about heading for Chaucer, making a 'pincer movement,' you said, reading in preparation . . ."

"Yes?"

"Well, I'm worried about that, you know. Chaucer was seriously influenced by Dante. And I hope you won't think I sound self-serving, but I really believe a better beginning would be to draw back—into medieval history. So much fine work has been done in this century, so many new questions asked, so many interesting answers hazarded—for instance, how the chance construction of a plow determines cultural attitudes for centuries, or how the moral fiber of a people can be dependent on the rainfall—you know, the whole matter of weather has been reopened!"

"Is that so!" said Celia, thrilled.

"And so what I've done is to make a list of several small paperbacks which I hope will give you both the great pleasure of an introduction into the new attempts at historical reconstruction, and provide a more or less firm footing . . ."

Eleven

It was an early evening party and it broke up when Philip took Francie and Nell to the bus. With him went Lily, who asked if it would be convenient to drive her home. As she lived on East Ninety-sixth Street, logistically speaking it was as convenient as, say, Detroit, and it took a long time before Philip was back again. Celia, whose mind had been powerfully concentrated by her own tastes and longings, and not her husband's, picked up the house and went off to bed. The next morning she woke confusedly refreshed and in a high state of amusement at the farfetched idea that she would be setting off by herself for France. Meanwhile, the most harassing of her problems was solved. Peter had handed her the list of books, which she had in turn handed to Philip as he left for a half-day downtown. Philip's office was a short walk from Scribners and Brentano's.

"Now is there anything else you need?" he had asked, a little puffy-looking.

"Good grief, what time did you finally get in?"

"Jesus, I don't know."

"Just the books."

"Well, I'll be back before two anyway. I don't seem to be able to get out of this meeting."

"Plenty of time. Just the books."

Philip went off to the subway leaving his wife in a fluttery, happy condition, but somehow the children failed to notice this. The three resident girls were at the breakfast table, uneasy, but eating—they ate through thick and thin—and Bess asked, "Are you very upset with daddy about the editorial?"

"Of course she isn't," said Polly soberly. "The whole point is to win. Francie said that Humphrey was the only one that could win. Isn't that right, mama?"

"No, it's not right. It'll tell you something about winning and losing that took my mind, Polly. There's an old man by the name of Leonard Woolf who's been writing his autobiography which is taking him quite a number of books, and I read that he plans to call the last one *The Journey Not the Arrival Matters*. And I thought, for heaven's sake, what an awkward, cumbersome title. Nobody will remember it. But you know, I can't forget it." Celia wrote out the title and pinned it on the bulletin board, and Polly got up to give it a good study. Isobel, who was very sentimental about her mother sighed, "Oh, mama," and began to cry. Her mother said, "For goodness' sake, it's not a sad thought! It's simply a very good philosophic way not to get yourself all beaten up and depressed! It lets you live as nobly as you care to try to live without fussing constantly because other people fail to be as fine and tiptop as you are. It lets you *laugh*, Bess."

"I *know* that! I love it," said Isobel, smiling and crying.

Harriet, who had lately adopted an observer's view of her family, broke her silence now. "I think you could say the same thing about Daddy, that what he's doing is just as noble and it's according to his conscience."

"Oh, absolutely, *of course*," said the mother, making everything all right again. They went to school.

The belief that plants, animals, and children cannot get on without the woman in the house was coming to an end as abruptly as the belief in progress. Celia would, nonetheless, have been helplessly anxious about worries subsumed, for instance, under *Household:* the future of the dark and light wash; under *Children:* getting braces off Bess's teeth and on to Polly's, the toppling of Harriet with the reentry of Francie and Nell, and no moderator; under *France:* no French, or at any rate no French the French knew; under *Flying:* Celia was afraid of the taking off and the landing of the aircraft; and finally under *Agnes Webb:* Celia was afraid of her mother. All of this would have made an agitating morning for her, but while mechanically she checked through the things that had to be done, her mind was given over to the thought of history and the historian, *the* historian. She could turn over and over again and with impunity Peter's conversation, his admiration. He was departing from her life as neatly as he had entered; he was returning to live abroad.

She was all set to go in a dress that was new, black ("I can't understand why you don't wear black with that hair," Jessie had said several times. "I guess you think black is for mourning."), the hem very short, a rope of paste pearls very long,—she could hang herself if they caught in her knee—when Philip came home without the books, and looking very guilty.

Philip was not guilty about forgetting the books, which he did not yet remember he had forgotten. Philip had crossed the line between wanting Lily and having her, and superbly sophisticated man that he believed himself to be, he was determined to seem normally thoughtful, and he transferred, for current domestic purposes, the source of guilt to the offending issue of *The State of the Union*, which he handed to Celia as he came through the door, as was his Monday habit. He now saw the Humphrey endorsement as the most welcome of red herrings, an unexpected turn of events, one of a series, certain to put Celia off the scent of Lily. For this impending clash (with his wife) over his Sad Duty (to the nation) he wore a sober mien.

Beneath this mien was considerable turmoil. The truth about this particular game of philandering was that left to his own devices Philip might have been content to pass his golden years playing it, content never to win. And if mores hadn't changed, or if everybody else's rules of behavior had remained faithful to what Philip believed they ought to be, he wouldn't have fallen. But Lily's mores were brand-new; she tripped him and he fell. In fact, it is not surprising that a man who has had such a history of right thinking and clean living to the age of fifty-two lacked the agility easily to suspend his conscience and to revel in a spell of transgression. The morning after it was a struggle for Philip not to feel sullied and ashamed, and he was truly bewildered that he had forfeited so fast and so finally the pleasure he took in his own superior moral character. The memory of the intense pleasure Lily gave him was in abeyance. He walked through his own door, feigning his ordinary self, the self when it was depressed or worried or defeated, the very self expected to walk through the door carrying *The State* with Humphrey's picture on the cover.

Celia scanned the outlines of Philip, clearly a man with no parcel, with no pocket bulges, with no books; and there rose up in her a sense of indignation, and there broke through her customary restraint not only the week's passion but resentment from the suddenly inflated grievances of recent years, so that her face took on quite a dramatic look of betrayal. And in a husky voice, the consequence of whispering her fury to keep the public out of it, she began, "You just treat me so *casually*. You make *too light* of my sense of worth, my dignity. Jesus God, a woman has to fight every day to believe she isn't a *farce*, the heroine of a *soap* opera . . ."

Philip was aghast and looked it. He had the breath knocked right out of him. He had nothing to say.

"My God, how you can be so insensitive, so *depreciative*, so indifferent to what is so *important* to me! My God, *everybody* wants to avoid living a cliché-ridden life."

He was aghast and baffled by how Celia could know about Lily, and he stared and waited. For her part, Celia was entirely unaccustomed to silence from Philip, entirely prepared for argument, rebuttal, and the launching of a jesuitical defense that would prove him wiser and better. She paused for it, and then realizing that he was stricken with attention, she gathered her wits with a rush to pursue her advantage.

"It's not only a matter of how *I'm* going to face the years ahead. You make a great mistake if you think it is. *You* have to face them too. Your father, after all, died at eighty-eight. There's no reason to think you'll get off the hook early."

Philip, who thought she was talking about the course of his repentance, was becoming unsteady on his feet. Celia was clutching *The State*, waving it about.

"This has been coming on for a long while, and in fact it is a commonplace in men in their middle years. I wonder you let yourself be so *trendy!*" Celia continued with a note of sarcasm, odd coming from her. "They just give into the temptation, these men, practically all the men we know— because it's *easy* and because it always seems sophisticated —they give into the temptation to be *cynical* instead of to *think*. Well, it's a very dubious proposition that men are in the hard world where all the facts are! and they're the ones who never read a book! Facts, facts, facts, really sometimes you sound like Mr. Gradgrind. I don't give a damn about *this!*" she said, flinging down *The State*. "I give a damn about *you*." Her sentimental sentence made her catch her breath. "Oh, Philip, I have such a stake in *growth*, in breaking through, transcending one's limitations —and I have it for *you*. Do you know one reason why I fell in love with you?"

Celia waited a moment for an answer from Philip, but he was suffering and mute (for the first time mute).

"Because you liked *Chopin* even though he was definitely *out*. You even liked *Tschaikovsky*. I thought it was so *courageous*. Do you want to know another reason why I fell in love with you? *Browning*. It was because you knew so much Browning. It would spill out of you, lines and lines of Browning . . . thread through your letters . . . and I, I was just nonplussed. I had nothing like that inside of me."

Another sociological fact surfaces here: Philip had gone

through public schools when there was still a lot of learning by rote, but Celia's education was private and called progressive, where memorizing was believed to be imitating. Instead, a child was encouraged to create his own poetry. It was the consequence of this to which she referred when she said, "I've never had the reservoir in my mind that you have—the *pool*—that I always thought you were so lucky to have, because from it one could become wiser and more reflective with all that wonderfully rich mental material to draw on, to add to. . . ." Her voice dropped and she added coldly, "And instead, what are you doing?"

Staggering, and he sat in the nearest chair. They were in the library, and he sat in Celia's chair. She stood.

"Contempt, sneering, that's what cynicism falls back on, instead of using the mind, instead of *thinking*. Do you know your mind's getting very closed, very rigid? How much, really, do you read of substance? All right, all right, you *can't*, you haven't the time—that's what all the men say—and I guess forgetting the books would be called a psychological defense—although *not by me*."

The wisp of a thought that Celia was not talking about his * * * with Lily was beginning to twist in Philip's rattled head.

"*I* think," she said, very severe now, "it's a case of chronic self-satisfaction. Your sympathetic understanding is becoming *atrophied*, that's what it really is. Your thoughts, your values—it's as though you learned what there is to learn at school, and the idea of moving beyond would be a breach of loyalty! I don't know how to talk to you anymore. If I come on something new, you say it's not new or it's wrong, and for a while I thought you had this stake in my being *dumber* and you *couldn't* listen to me. But you can't listen to *anybody* . . ."

And true enough, Philip was not listening now. He was recovering.

". . . so that I would be a source for *you too*, a place to come to and be refreshed and restored." Celia stopped for a second to cry. She had touched her own heart and almost mechanically the tears spilled, as happens to women, but it doesn't mean anything. Celia stopped crying as quickly as she'd started: "It isn't only the books. When was the last time we had an easy *exchange* about anything?" She took a breath and then began again reflectively, "I don't know when your thoughts began coming *down* from *above*. Because you've set up to be my judge. Somewhere, you got very elevated! I bring *up* things with you like a *craven petitioner*—the money I gave to M-L, for instance. Well, why in the name of God should I get myself into a bind about using money that is just as much mine as yours? I don't niggle about the money *you* spend. I find it intolerable at forty-five to be cross-examined and scolded like a child. I know it's my fault for letting it go on, I know it. Well, I'm through."

Not with the monologue, however. Philip said, "Don't worry about the money," weakly, in an attempt to be soothing. He had automatically resumed listening because the subject was money.

"I'm *not* worried about the money! Do you think I'm worried about money? That's what I mean. You don't hear what I'm saying. You listen so *selectively*. I mean, when we were talking about the girls, about Francie . . . where she was spending the night?" Celia's voice climbed again as she remembered another irritation. "You know, you don't like your old illusions disturbed, even when they were illusions in the first place. You want to believe that I had a reverence for my own virgin condition, but actually I thought it was *sophisticated*, it was a mark of worldly independence, to have a love affair—which was still a very romantic notion in those days. But today the whole thing is *much grubbier*. You worry about the woolly mammoth. I already see myself needing to protect *Harrie*, to give her the moral support she needs so that she doesn't sleep with somebody before she *wants* to. Tennie said the other night I was Mrs. Bennet and you act as though I really am, only not doing so well as she did and I ought to take a leaf out of her book." She paused. "I'm *light years* from Mrs. Bennet, because the children are. Light years!"

There was another pause, and then she ordered sternly, "Take Lily! You can't make head or tail of her!"

This was simply not so, thought Philip, and he really rallied, and said quietly, "I do listen to Lily . . . and I am listening to you," and as if to prove it, he didn't argue, didn't offer a rebuttal. "I'm very sorry, very sorry I let myself pay so little attention to . . . to you . . . to the things that concern you . . . the books."

And it was proof.

Twelve

ORDERLY, civil, responsible people have a pace so engrained that their upheavals may appear calculated since they invariably subside in time for the next thing on the schedule. At 1:45 Celia lost her self-control, but she had regained it by 3:00, leaving an hour to tend to last-minute details without rushing. The girls drifted home from school to find a mother calmly checking off a list and a father calmly putting a few dishes in the dishwasher; and each child took one minute to see something was the matter. Their dismay had the effect of making them thoughtful and tidy, and wonderfully behaved at the airport where politely they took turns checking the Flight Delayed sign for four hours. With each of these hours the possibility grew that the connection to Marseilles could not be made. The mother appeared unannoyed. The father gave no advice or instructions. The children had fixed smiles.

Bess, who had the least intolerance for family discord, nudged her father: "Don't you think mama looks beautiful?"

"Yes, I do," said the father, solemnly. He didn't recognize her.

Finally Celia was off, and the next day Philip and the girls woke in varying conditions of holiday cheer for a stretch of life without her. *Mirabile dictu* and haply, the prospect for Philip seemed much gayer than it had been the morning before. In the first place he was feeling safe, and in the second, young. The essence of Celia's dour indictment, boiled down, was that he didn't listen to anybody, that he might start by listening to Lily; and by a marvelous coincidence, he had. Lily told him a lot of the same things Celia did, when he was in a better position to take them in. So he began his sojourn in a kind of larky mood of release, which was not destined to be sustained, alas. Upon his next visit to Lily immediately he began learning more than he had bargained for.

Necessarily, Lily had a pad, although it was actually somebody else's.

"I'm really strict with myself about collecting stuff. All my worldly goods in a backpack, that idea. So I move from sublet to sublet. Itchy feet."

Intent upon absorbing the meaning of every word, Philip propped himself on an elbow to look down the length of Lily to her feet. They did not look scaly.

"As a matter of fact, I'm just as glad Tennie turned me down because I've been in New York long enough. Time to move on."

"Tennie . . . ?" It was from this point the course of studies began.

"Actually, I *thought* Tennie simply might not have the flexibility to recognize something really nice when it was offered. And I was right. But I was wrong about you."

Lily was on her elbow now, and smiled fondly down at him. Philip was off his elbow and lay flat because of his bursitis. He was amazed by her charming candor and detachment; he understood that he was an ace in the hole.

Her very words: "Always have an ace in the hole, as my father would say. I must have taken that advice to heart. I'm quite good at looking after myself. As a matter of fact I have a job lined up in would-you-believe Boston?"

"Boston?"

"They've got a couple of very respectable trade houses up there, you know, not counting the university presses."

"When would you leave?"

"Well, that's it. I was so damn pissed off I nearly walked out Wednesday, and I may just . . . you know, Tennie *talks* a radical line but *viscerally* he isn't where it's at, if you'll excuse my criticizing a blood relation. You want to know what he said to me once? I was trying to get him to take a study on where women go after they get a graduate degree—the answer is no place—and he hedged and stalled and finally he said, 'Man's love is of man's life a thing apart,/'Tis woman's whole existence.' That's where he's at! *Splat* in the middle of the Byronic *mentalité*. Talk about what's culturally determined!"

Try as he might, Philip did not know what she meant.

"I mean," she said helpfully, "that's what Woman's Liberation is all about. All the suppositions of the last two or three hundred years will have to be rethought, and it's lucky one-half the human race will be coming at it fresh. For example, obviously the ethics of whom you sleep with is up for reconsideration. And it's the women who are going to set the new standards. For my part, I would not go to bed with anybody I didn't love."

Philip did not harbor the illusion that Lily's love was of the same dimension as was the old True Love, notwithstanding that like the old True Love the course would not run smooth. Impersonally, indifferently, events throughout the world were militating against the success of this private sally. Primary among these were the increasingly violent confrontation between the police and students in the Latin Quarter, the possibility of unrest spreading through the whole of France, and that Celia would be in danger. Philip could not get in touch with his wife.

Celia had gone off to France on Monday. In Wednesday's mail there was a postcard from Agnes which, to do her justice, was mailed three weeks previously and in plenty of time. It was in response to the earlier proposed visit in June. "Sweetie—Second thoughts! Come in September. Reprieve from the doctors! Off to visit friends. Phone service disrupted. Call when settled. A." Agnes had a cable style with postcards as though she were charged by the word. Philip felt a clutch at his stomach, said to himself, "She's a big girl. She can take care of herself." But on Friday morning when he left his office to walk over to Heavensgate to talk to Tennie, he was a distracted man. Among other things he was certainly nervous about what Tennie knew, given Lily's delightfully open style, but Tennie didn't give a sign of knowing.

"The thing is," said Philip, wearing the hat of the harried husband, "she doesn't really know any French. And there's nobody over there who can spare the time to track her down. They're tracking down de Gaulle. They got through once and spoke to the concierge and she said Madame was *en vacances*."

Tennie looked long and passively at Philip and said

finally, "I'm not sure I take your meaning, old buddy. You mean poor Celia may be wandering from Aix to Arles to Avignon with nobody to look *after?* Or do you mean poor Celia with nobody to tell her what to look *at?*"

"Don't be a damn fool, Tennie! Do you realize flights to Orly are being rerouted? You have to go to Brussels or you have to go down to Turin or Milan?"

"Well, if you want to know what I think, I think your response to this business is *inappropriate*—to borrow a phrase my shrink is fond of. I don't say it isn't typical, but it's inappropriate," said Tennie in a tone that was fond and had the effect of calming Philip for about a day.

Back to Lily, who in the matter of appetites had a disproportionate interest in eating. Since she did not cook, a lot of Philip's instruction was conducted over the white linen cloths of better French restaurants. "You see," she said, "nineteenth-century capitalism was *labor*-intensive. They needed every ounce of the worker's energy. That's why they put the interdict on *carnal pleasures*. But now that we have a *capital*-intensive economy it simply leaves everybody with *too much time*. They get restless. So they've had to lift the ban on sex. But people can't live *banlessly*. They feel they have to have some little thing to torment themselves into order, so they've checked out the deadly sins and they found gluttony and they said everybody's got to go on a *diet*. So this whole bloody country's obsessed with being overweight . . ."

Lily was a weekday affair, strenuous physically as well as mentally. Philip had the weekend to rest up, had he been able. But by Saturday Celia was not the only one missing. No de Gaulle! No word from either, and Philip's distraction about the two grew to such proportions as to produce a third distraction—that his relationship with Lily would enter, on Monday, a humiliating phase. Once this third idea came into his head it was a real horserace in there. Meanwhile violence had broken out in Strasbourg, Rennes, Nantes, and Grenoble.

At home, the children thought their pleasure was their father's chief problem, especially as he would come upon one of them, say, "Let's see. What do you think we ought to do?" and walk out of the room. As it happened, they didn't do anything that weekend because Philip had to stay within reach of the phone, although until Sunday, only Marian called to ask about Celia, and got moaning and groaning for her pains. Then on Sunday noon there was a call for Philip. It was Peter Jacobs.

"I just talked to Tennie. He says you're worried about not hearing from your wife, and he thought I might be some help. I fly to Milan tonight, and if you give me her mother's number and address I'd be absolutely delighted to try to track her down. I've got some time to kill, as it happens."

Jacobs could not have been warmer in his assurances to Philip—how handy Italy was to France, and so on—that he would not find such an errand a trouble. Philip, bewildered by the willingness of anybody to go so far out of the way, was nonetheless very grateful to him.

"Good idea of yours to send Jacobs chasing after Celia," said Philip to his brother. It was into the next week, and Philip affected a nonchalance about anything he wanted to know, as usual. In addition to Celia Philip was now missing Lily. De Gaulle, however, had been found in Romania exhorting its people to be more grand.

"I didn't send Jacobs after Celia. I told him you were

worried about where she was. But I thought you'd pegged him for Lily so I asked him how was that going? He said she was too young for him. He needed a grown-up. Well, I said anyway she seems to have wandered off."

"Who? Lily?"

"No, Celia. Don't you remember you lost Celia? Frankly I don't think of Lily as a loss. I let her quit so I wouldn't have to fire her." Tennie sounded confident that Philip knew Lily had left Heavensgate.

"I didn't know she stopped working," said Philip in a voice that had the ring of truth.

"I thought she'd talk to you about it . . . give you her version. Matter of fact, I was having some misgivings about Lily . . . leading her on you know. But she'll be all right, that baby. She knows how to even the score." Tennie gave Philip a look of ambiguous meaning. Philip did not hazard a comment. Tennie continued, "She's not only got herself a cozy new situation—she'll probably be taking two or three of our authors along with her—at least one of whom we'll be sorry about. What a nice bold ruthless girl she is. I'll miss her. But you know that boundless energy, that imaginative vitality, it's exhausting if you have it all day long. An occasional lunch, swell. But I can certainly see what Peter means. Better to go questing after somebody restful like Celia."

"Jesus, it really relieves my mind, Jacobs looking out for her. You know, they figure a force of 50,000 in Paris alone. Thirty thousand flics and another 20,000 riot police. That's a lot of vicious people. And now, God alone knows, with the general strike . . ."

Philip's anguish was certainly not unwarranted. He spent three nights in a row with his motherless children—

McDonald's, Pizza Palace, Howard Johnson's—this parental performance in lieu of Lily, and it was ruining his stomach. On Thursday morning she called.

"Well, I'm back! But just to get my gear! But I want to see you. I'd just hate flying off without even a good-by!" And that evening, sitting naked, cross-legged, unselfconscious on the bed like a child, and never more animated, she said, "You must think I'm terribly egocentric, and you're right, but it's a really cushy moment for somebody like me. And I've got a million ideas. I mean things are going to be opening up. Everybody's going to need a Company Woman. It's a seller's market. And frankly it was a real blow—Heavensgate. But it forced me to reexamine the options, and for instance, I thought over book reviewing for you—I really gave it serious consideration," she said earnestly, wanting Philip to know that he was not passed over lightly, "but the fact is there's too much ephemera in journalism. I need something to build on. I think this thing in Boston is going to be good, really good. I just want to be in the right spot to be poised to strike . . ."

Tubby the cobra. So that seemed to be the end of that, and they kissed good-by, Philip a wiser man.

Part Two

The French Rebellion

Thirteen

I n France every single one of the possible dangers to Celia's well-being, as feared by Philip, escaped her notice. She entered upon her sojourn in a grand psychological state. Her burst of fury against her husband could not have been better-timed, since it left her lightheaded, empty of years of assorted marital grievances. All her American anguish dropped like a stone, and all the French anguish proceeded without her, owing to her ignorance of the language. She moved in a private nimbus from plane to plane, from bus to bus, unruffled by delays and missed connections, and finally arrived by taxi at her mother's door with a day lost in transit. There was nobody to know the difference. It is not such a farfetched phenomenon that a woman at the crux of the much-admired extended family, implicit in the lives of all the members, included in all the schemes—that such a woman who is abruptly translated to a condition of having nobody to account to, nobody to account for—should find it very winning. And although it is true that May is the best month for the Bronx, it is very nice on the

Mediterranean as well. The evidence of Cézanne is every-where; every roof tile, every leaf.

It was a sunny Wednesday morning, instead of a sunny Tuesday afternoon, when Celia coolly took the curves of the coastal range from Marseilles to La Ciotat, at the back of a bus, and a knot of panic did not begin to form in her stomach until the five-minute zigzag ride up the side of the busy, flowering, fish-filled town to the house in which Agnes had her flat. The concierge, who at first did not rec-ognize Celia without children, greeted her with a barrage of scolding language, and Celia, who had enough school French to ask the questions she wanted to know, did not have enough to understand the answers. Everything had to be repeated, with gestures.

"Four francs, seventy"—the hands of the cabman whack-ing the air, fingers splayed.

And then, "Ah, your mother would be astonished, she had not the least idea you would come until the fall. The doctors in Marseilles have shrugged their shoulders. Her friends came on Sunday to take her off. She is descended for the month at Quissac . . ." And Mme Convenable, the concierge, for whom sympathetic concern was the farthest cry, found an address and phone number for Celia, handed her the house keys, shrugged her own shoulders, and dis-appeared.

When Celia understood there would be no mother to greet, her stomach unknotted, her head reemptied, and she glided up the stairs in spite of her bags. The apartment was closed up and dark. Still with her coat on, she went to the windows, and the unaccustomed and foreign act of open-ing shutter after shutter into the full air, throwing them back wide against the outside wall, hearing the clap and the click, while the amazing yellow light filled the rooms, left her stunned, mind and heart. It is the lot of an American woman, after all, usually to feel for a wall switch, to be screened by screens.

There were three rooms, one very ample, serving for a studio, and giving out to a balcony that overlooked the red rooftops and tiered streets of the town, the cranes from the shipyards fringing the bottom and the blue Mediterranean beyond. There was a small back bedroom, and a small kitchen. The charm and mark of Agnes were lying pell-mell everywhere in the form of scarves, shawls, throws, pillows, and pottery—terracotta blue and white, terracotta green and white—oil canvases and prints, books in French and English, the bathroom full of facepaint pots, the kitchen of seasonings and jams. For whatever reason she had left Morris Webb, it could not have been the need for a more orderly existence. The Duponts, on their rare visits, came *en famille* and were accustomed to put up at Le Rose Thé in La Ciotat-Plage. Celia had never slept in her mother's house. Her spirits now expanded into these rooms without a qualm and indeed with a free-winging sense of proprietorship and entitlement; of having at least the right for the present to fill up all the space her mother had temporarily abandoned.

Although Celia must call Agnes.

But first she must change from the black dress and pearls, bathe, unpack a little, be hungry (but it was noon and the shops were closing) nap instead, wake up and venture out into the streets to buy, to demand (her best verbs), bread, cheese, oranges, coffee, butter, wine (her best nouns), count her change (her worst problem), and continue, carrying her purchases in her mother's string bag, to saunter through the market streets and have her elbows brushed by rather fierce fellow housewives in their black cardigans, breasting the sidewalks, an amazing number looking like the handsome Anna Magnani. Every other shop was a fish stall with fish whole, fish eyes, fillets, eels, and everywhere baskets filled with squid, their slithery pink tentacles spilling over the wicker. She bought flowers, another of her nouns, but pointed to the pastry, and on balance thought she was already getting a feeling for the language.

It is also a commonplace for an American woman to find in the open markets of a small European town, in the lettuces out of the earth, the breads out of the oven, possibly even in squid, the terrible evidence of how much has been lost to her, how removed she is from the reality of the soil, the seasons, how enviable are the lots of the women of these provincial worlds. The bread, the cheese, a bottle of the local wine, rosé but not sweet, combined to cast in Celia the illusion that she had rejoined a simpler, more elemental self, unspoken for, untied, untugged by the exigencies of others. She was certainly intoxicated, did not call her mother, and slept like a top.

The next morning she got up and opened all the shutters and continued the simple life, making coffee in the simple kitchen (which had an electric stove, refrigerator, and hot and cold water just like the complicated kitchen), and then she finished off the second foot of last night's bread with butter and jam while sitting on the balcony, musing at the colors of the sky and the sea. She was certainly not taxing her mind. Along about noon she went down to the concierge, for whom she had prepared, "Pardon me, where is the car of my mother, please?" was told, didn't understand, was taken a little roughly by the arm to it and given the keys. Mme Convenable remained uninterested in Celia and her plight, or if she had a plight. Celia was intimidated by people who did not want to like her, however superfluous their affection was, as for instance, stewardesses on planes. It was because she would have had to approach Mme Convenable to put the call through that Celia deferred phoning her mother.

With a pat to the hood of the car, and a mere sketch of a thought that she might save herself the phone call by driving to Quissac, wherever that might be, Celia set off on foot for town again. It was her purpose this time to buy more things to eat, and also a phrase book with the words "fill 'er up" in it. She came home instead with a heavy, hardback French-English dictionary pressed upon her as a better choice by the clerk at the stationers who *did* like her— she could make a list of her own phrases, he said, cheering her on—and with a pâté de campagne, salad greens, and two more bottles of the rosé. She was spreading out.

And the next thing Celia did—and after very little thought, considering how pivotal the act—was to take her first committed step into the third third of her life. She picked from among her mother's books a small Maigret paperback, a whodunit, and took her first steps into what would become a hot pursuit of the French language. Laboriously but happily she began to track it down. In less than a week she would reach page 25.

And it was either Saturday or Sunday or Monday that Celia added further to her self-intoxicated, elemental existence by incorporating the use of the stick-shift car. She decided to drive to Aix, and if she did not kill anybody, she would then proceed to Quissac by a roundabout route, passing through parts of Provence she had missed on earlier visits.

The trip to Aix was quite thrilling owing to the fascination of working the gears. For a while the road was called la Route des Crêtes, which is accurately described as fairly steep, "runs along the highest cliffs in France," and gets three stars for its panoramic view. By not looking at this view Celia arrived without incident at la place de la Libération, and well-named it was. She stepped out on to the pavement a highly charged and unencumbered girl. By levitation or by regression she had completed her liberation, as it seemed, from the burden of her whole adult history. Husband, children, responsibilities—her mind was clear of the lot. She sauntered slowly up one side and down the other of the beautiful cours Mirabeau, passed the mossy fountains, spreading her custom among bookshops and cafés, kindly pressing to the wall, smiling, when swarms of shouting students, arms linked, took over the sidewalk. She bought a sketchpad, a French grammar, Michelin road maps 80, 83, and 84. She had an omelet and white wine on the way and pastry on the return, and just before she left, at the height of her transport, she bought the three-volume Pléiade edition of Proust at a sobering seventy-five francs.

About a week had now passed since Celia had been obliged to give a serious thought to the welfare of another human being, and in that week she very nearly achieved knowing a paradisiac existence. After the excursion to Aix she went to bed in the full flush of it, but the next day, opening the shutters to another sunny morning, there was the tiny serpent of a thought that the elemental life, as well as the sophisticated one, is liable to be boring without companionship. And the idea of Peter Jacobs, about whom she thought constantly, and which contributed significantly to the delirious quality of her reveries, as well as to her choice of French instead of, for instance, Sanskrit—that idea of being with him began to turn more taunting. As she studied the map with a pen lining the route through Les Baux, Pont du Gard, Aigues-Mortes, Stes.-Maries-de-la-Mer, St.-Gilles, she did not experience the longing usually induced by the very names. And when she went resolutely down to market for the cheese and bread for her trip, she found herself overcome by a craving for fish—to buy the fish, to prepare it, smell it cooking, eat it with somebody else.

There was a large shopping bag in the kitchen bearing the legend, "Mettez un tigre dans votre moteur," and Celia was putting into it the picnic, and her several books, guides, and maps, when the concierge knocked, and rattled off an announcement that was Greek to Celia, a deflating linguistic experience. She stood at the door, with her face vacant, her mind struggling to translate, when a figure loomed up out of the shadows of the stairwell, and said, "So you're all right, after all," and there was Peter Jacobs, a miracle of transmutation from mind to matter, with a crafty and happy look of achievement which became his capuchin face. Mme Convenable shrugged her shoulders and retired.

Jacobs, in a tan sweater and corduroy trousers, came in as though he had just happened by, but he said, "Good God, woman, whatever possessed you to keep a mother in this place! Everybody else keeps them in Florida. The airports are closed. I had to rent a car in Milan. Christ, what a hassle. If your husband hadn't gotten in such a flap about your wandering into the cross fire of the revolution, I would have given up pursuit of you altogether. That's how bad it got. But I promised I'd find you dead or alive. And how the hell we're going to get a cable out to him with the strike . . ."

"Oh, for heaven's sake! What *is* all his fussing about!" Celia said. Through the buzzing in her ears from the blood rushing through her empty head, there darted a moment's pique at Philip, at the reach of the long arm of Philip. "Why should anything be the matter? He knows I'm with my mother!" She laughed, so to speak, reasonably.

"Of course, he's outrageous, but he thinks you aren't."

"Well, now, why does he think that?"

"Because she wrote to say she wouldn't be here. Is she?"

"As a matter of fact, no."

"That's a point for his side, then. Do you know where she is?"

"I know where she is, but she doesn't know where I am. What do you mean revolution? I've never been in such a peaceful place."

"I myself couldn't see you were in danger, but Philip . . . and since I was going to be in the neighborhood, I just volunteered."

"I thought you had begun your sabbatical. I thought you were some place in Italy. I didn't expect to see you again," she said instead of, "I thought I was perfectly safe."

"Well, the thing is, I've been worried about your third third, you see. So I've come out of a sense of responsibility, urged on, you might say, to see you start off properly. Philip was anxious I bring you something to read, and I've brought you a couple of books. He said something about losing the list . . ."

"What do you mean revolution?"

Peter told her how it was progressing, that a general strike was called, which might make a cable difficult, and she listened as though it were taking place in Siam, said vaguely there was some milling around in Aix and down at the shipyards, "*les chantiers*, one of my countless new nouns! You know, actually, I've thought about you a great deal, Peter. You made quite a serious impression on . . . well, for instance, it had never occurred to me before our talk that rainy night in . . . that I might do *French*. Well, and I've begun! I've got a new dictionary, a grammar, *Maigret en Vacances* for my text, and I'm rattling along at a great rate, more than a page an hour. And my vocabulary is something criminal—bloodstains, handcuffs, fingerprints. If I ever get in trouble with the French police we can have a really good talk. . . ." She was on a zigzag course to cover her confusion, stopped abruptly, changed subjects, pulled out her maps, and said she was just heading off into the country for a few days on the way to see her mother.

Peter sat down beside her to look over her maps, his enthusiasm easily enlisted—it was wonderful country, perfect time of the year, how he envied her—and then all of a sudden it occurred to him that Philip might be right after all, that maybe there was reason to be concerned about violence.

"Oh, I'm going to keep strictly to rural areas. Once I get out of here I'm not taking any red routes. Only yellow."

Well, and what a coincidence, he said, because he'd brought her just the book, one of the most fascinating, wonderfully written—"The origins of French agriculture. Where you'll find the longest furrows, which system of crop rotation was used and why. Everything! Bloch's *French Rural History*. You won't want to put it down, once you get into it. Of course it's a little esoteric for the beginner. You know, Celia, the best thing would be to have somebody guide you."

Celia certainly had seen the suggestion in the offing, and that it was out of the question, and that she would have to say firmly no. She said, "Well, yes, you know it really would be awfully nice to have a little company, but," she added in haste to correct a wrong inference, "the nights— the nights I must really dedicate to my French."

"Of course, I would be glad to be your pony."

"That would not be moral. I must ride it out myself."

Peter caught the local branch of the telecommunications syndicate between strikes and sent a cable: CELIA FINE ALL WELL JACOBS.

Fourteen

I̲T̲ was nearly dark before they reached Les Baux. Through the first hours Celia sat aghast on her side, "What have I done! What have I done!" running on a tape through her head. They cleared the coastal range and the outreaches of Marseilles, stopping to pick up some things,—a sketchbook for Peter, prosciutto and pâté—everything friendly, very loose: she feeling, regardless, tight as a tick. But she was not, after all, eighteen, and when they entered the variegated farmland between the Durance and the Rhône, the countryside began to draw her out, and she was quite turned about by the time they lay their picnic. It was by the ruins of a small chapel, "Romanesque, 10th c., built on the site of a temple to Diana." Although this site got only a thin red line on the map, and no commendation for panoramic view, it had one nonetheless; of mildly undulating land, small, irregular fields, some vineyard, some olive, some under the plow, all made neat by hedgerows, by tall reed windscreens, a line here of poplars, there of plane trees.

And the color was the color of Van Gogh. In the middle distance there was a farmstead.

"Don't you think it's *unjust*," Celia said musing—she had been turning up a lot of neutral subjects—"that we see the beauty of these fields *because* of Van Gogh, instead of the other way around?"

They were sitting in the tallish grass, propped against the ruin, finishing the wine from two wine glasses out of Celia's mother's kitchen.

"It's just another homely truth," Peter said. "The more you know about something the more interesting it is. Now I look at a farmhouse like that, and I think, that's where the good life is. But . . . well, there's a line in Chekhov, in *The Three Sisters*, where one of them is asked why she is so moody, so disconsolate, so unable to settle down in their town. 'It's 700 miles from Moscow!' she says. And that's what I remember whenever I find myself tempted to buy some rustic little . . . I remember that I do not want to be 700 miles from people who can understand what I'm thinking about. I've got to have a peer around, or better, a peeress." He smiled at Celia, with a reference to the dangling implications.

Celia smiled but let them dangle. She said, "You'd think it would be easy enough to solve by getting the peeress on to the farm with you, but I've just read something a bit discouraging. It seems there is a disproportionately high number of bachelors among French farmers. The women don't like the hard, lonely life. The percentage of farm girls who go to the city is huge, and the percentage of city girls who marry farmers is too small to put on their graph. A sociologist's nightmare. I suppose French girls all read Chekhov and are warned off."

"Of course if they knew more about the absorbing cultural implications of the irregular open-field system, examples of which are spread out before you . . ."

"Oh, no question! Turn *anybody* on to the hard, lonely life!"

"You laugh now, but wait until you find out about the long furlong and the wheeled plow."

At the end of the afternoon, when they were approaching Les Baux, there were massive black clouds building, and the great prow of rock, so dramatic of itself, was wildly lighted by the forming of the storm. It had the effect, as Celia remarked, that was striven for in the first scene of Hamlet. "This bodes some strange eruption to our state," Peter responded hopefully. And the two players made mad by the ominous sky hastened to drive up to the ancient town, without taking their dinner at the only three-star restaurant likely to fall in their way.

Celia, squinting to read the Michelin guide in the eerie light, asked, "What does *merle* mean?"

"Blackbird."

"What does *grive* mean?"

"Thrush."

"Good grief! We've just missed mousse of blackbird! We've just missed mousse of thrush!"

But they ate well, and roamed the stormy promontory until the rains drove them in, each to his own room. At the door of hers, Peter, who had pointedly kept at arm's length, said rather severely, "Is it *reasonable* to expect passion on such idyllic terms in such a setting to be resisted? Is it *moral?*"

Celia, feeling like a foolish virgin, gave him a silly, apologetic smile and slipped through her door. In her room she failed to put in her hour of study. For quite a while she leaned through the casement into the storm, until she was sopping wet and finally had to close the shutters. She picked about her spare quarters, examining its few amenities—the doilies, the bolster, the interesting ideas in the bathroom—and she was even able to make out the sign on the back of the door, which began, roughly translated, "In case of conflagration in your room, keep your sang-froid, don't cry out 'Fire!' " A timely warning. The next morning she threw open her shutters to a sky washed clean, the sun shining on the chain of peaks, the ravines still a midnight blue. After breakfast they set out for Pont du Gard.

Beneath the ancient aqueduct the river was high from the spring rains, the woods a spring green, and the banks steep and slippery, and in order to set out a picnic, or prop a sketchbook, it was necessary in some way to find purchase with one's foot on the tough root of a tree. One even had to hang on to a branch to pass the wine bottle. However, for several hours they never thought to look for a safer spot, and they never fell into the river. The river was about five feet below them, and at the edge of it two rats soon appeared. It is testimony to the idyllic place, and the idyllic things they were doing—eating, drinking, counting the arches of the Pont du Gard, drawing them, scattering them with artistic leafy branches, all the while carrying on an absorbing conversation—that Celia, after some uncertain minutes, thought the rats were not too bad-looking for rats. They were brown for one thing, and for another they never actually gnashed their teeth.

"It is not only the rats who are an unexpected pleasure," said Celia. She wanted to acknowledge her initial mistrustfulness and her present happiness. "I never would have managed so well on my own. Certainly I wouldn't have found the Gigondas." They had moved from the humble wine of the region to the best. "You've been all through here before, haven't you?" she said.

"Years ago, with my first wife. We were living in Verona, and we drove up for a couple of weeks."

"May I ask how many wives you've had?"

"Two. Only two. It doesn't seem an awful lot."

"That's odd. Only one husband seems an awful lot." She sighed, whether for the homely truth or for the indiscretion. They were becoming quickly very intimate, verbally.

Peter said after a moment, "You don't think of getting out?"

"Think of it?" she laughed. "I *think* of it and I think I won't. I like the family story. You know S. V. Hume? She's a novelist?"

"I know who she is, but I've never read her books."

"Well, she wouldn't be surprised. She says the people she writes for have two fixed habits. One is they don't read fiction, and the other is they don't buy hardbacks. So she has to teach. She's become a sort of friend. We found ourselves sitting together one night in the back row of a fund-raising business for McCarthy—both of us political diffidents, flushed out. Anyway, she writes a sort of contemporary comedy of manners, and she'd been having a stagnant spell, and her cleaning lady, wanting to cheer her on, told her, 'You ought to write a family story. Everybody likes a family story.' "

"And you like a family story."

"Yes, I like to live it. But you have to pay for it. And I suppose in the good capitalist tradition, you get what you pay for."

"Not many people seem to think it's worth the candle anymore."

"That's true. There are certainly times when it's hard not to have doubts. I just read a review of Miss Hume's new book coming over. It was in last week's *State of the Union*, and do you know who did the review? Lily! And she thought it was *awful*. She said it was about the sort of marital wheeling and dealing that was dependent upon the cultivation of underlying sadomasochistic tendencies, and so on—people are no longer willing to submit to this sort of perversion—something like that. It's one way to sum it up, I suppose."

Peter was thoughtful for a minute and then asked, "Is *now* one of the times when you have doubts?"

"Oh, Peter," she sighed again. "I'm just doubt-*ridden*. You must know . . . I root about trying to . . . retrieve my reasons for . . . *constancy*, but at the moment, I can't remember *any*." She laughed.

"That's the spirit!" he said, and he gave her time.

They sketched on. In a little while Peter suggested, "Instead of getting out altogether you might slip out now and again."

"That's just what Jessie recommends. She couldn't be more pro-libido, especially since she's taking courses. It would be terrifically satisfying to her if I slipped out, for the *clinical* interest."

"Save yourself and at the same time serve the social sciences!"

"I already am serving the social sciences. I'm seeing if monogamy is a Viable Alternative!"

"God Almighty, I think you deserve a government grant.

There aren't a lot of people who still find sex a matter for conscience-wracking."

"Well, if you want to know, I'm embarrassed by it—although I don't know whether I'm ashamed to be left behind by the world . . . or ashamed of the world."

From Pont du Gard they skirted Nîmes for fear of the insurrection, and headed south to the sea, to pass the night at the walled medieval town of Aigues-Mortes. By night Celia felt more absurd than she did by day, a ridiculous Pamela, 200 years past her prime. At dinner she returned Peter's avowal of love, with qualifications: "I don't pretend to be more virtuous than the next person. It's a private pact . . . Hannah Arendt talks about a dialogue with the self . . . or, I'm too old, too inflexible. I grew up in a household where there weren't any women, only the sternest sexual decorum."

In the course of time the sediment deposited by the tides stranded Aigues-Mortes several kilometers inland. To walk barefoot on the beach one has to get into the car and drive over. Alluvial action was as exciting as the wheeled plow to Peter and hence to Celia. He could not talk enough about it, and she could not hear enough. It is surprising how the subject lent itself to the exchange of their tangled feelings. For a while they walked on the beach, and then they drove at random on little roads through the grand emptiness of the marsh, rarely passing another car, sometimes catching sight of a grazing troupe of the Camargue wild horses, in a calm moment, it seemed. Once in the middle of nowhere the road ended at a river, and they had to wait for a ferry for an extra hour because it was lunchtime. So they sat on the edge of the bank with their own picnic and tried to record the sense of immensity in their sketchbooks, but failed.

At Stes. Maries-de-la-Mer Celia bought a doormat made of woven hemp from a gypsy. The feast day of the gypsies' favorite saint, Sara, had two or three nations of them gathered, against a dozen tourists. The nations had a great interest in Celia. From other gypsies she bought several silver rings and chains for her daughters.

"I couldn't have borne leaving them if Philip weren't such an excellent father. He adores them and they adore him. He makes life very safe for them—for all of us."

Celia and Peter were having coffee at a table out of doors, under a hazy sky, just across from the ninth-century fortress church. Peter said, "But *you* don't adore him."

After a pause, Celia said, "No. It's a fallow time . . . but like your fields, regrowth is implicit, it's underlying. And it isn't that I don't mind, but . . . I guess I don't really *worry*, you know."

"You don't worry that Philip will look around for somebody to . . . cultivate, so to speak?"

She laughed, had a tender thought for Philip and his moral fences and shook her head. "I don't think I'd even begrudge it. I just wouldn't want to know about it. Oh, Peter, Peter," she said, after taking a deep breath, "I'm really riven. I'm on the one hand so *happy*, so unexpectedly in love with life . . . in love with you [third sigh], and on the other I see myself as clearly irresponsible,—inexcusably *girlish* in inviting your . . . in not coming through. . . . It humiliates me to think I'm simply an aging tease. But I want you to know that I don't worry about betraying Philip—somehow, I don't know why—but to betray *you*, that worries me a lot. The thing is, it's not a matter of Philip or you. It's you or me. And for me, well, I feel myself from birth to death sort of an expanding web—did you know I was born Cecilia Agnes Webb?—and my values are too intricately spun, too intricately knotted, over too long a time, I guess."

Given Celia's age and a sensual hunger at least a little appeased by learning the history of transhumance along the Mediterranean littoral, it is not all that remarkable that she was able to resist Peter. After all, Peter was not absolutely irresistible. Now in his mid-fifties, he had turned up in Celia's life at a time when he was panicky, and ricocheting between denial that he was over the hill physically and denial that he was intellectually spent. Notwithstanding his panache in respect to the first denial, it was in the second that he had a greater stake. He was feeling crowded by a rising group of younger scholars. Celia's admiration for his mind, his accomplishments, her unaffected absorption in what he was thinking about, rearoused his own interest in his own material. An excited listener was what he needed badly. That he needed it more than an excited sexual response he would be the last to admit.

And so, willy-nilly Peter was suspended by Celia in a lingering state of leisurely peace he had not often known. He found himself freed to talk about his own life, about Marina, his first wife—or as he thought of her, his real wife —how they'd been unintimidated, freewheeling, the two of them early pioneers in what was subsequently to be called the New Life-Style, both successful, both publishing, he in English, she in Italian in Rome. When finally it came to reasons why they should stay together, there was no literature on the subject, no precedents. As to the other women with whom he had had close dealings, the satisfactions were nice but ephemeral, and one day when he looked back and thought he had nothing to add up, he got frightened, and married Janet, who had been his student.

He said to Celia, "The only women who left me with a sense of guilt, of having seriously transgressed, of having *sinned* . . . are the two I did right by, married fair and square."

The fourth morning was understood to be the last morning of unaccountability. They had spent the night at a simple hotel near St. Gilles, too simple. Now they were sitting on a curbstone sketching the curious façade of its remarkable church. St. Gilles was one of those numerous eastern Mediterranean saints who were inspired to get into barques without oar or sail, leaving themselves to the will of the waves, and getting brought in this manner to Provence. A remarkable number made this journey. The three portals were a quarry of detail much beyond the capabilities of either Celia or Peter, and Peter, showing wear from such an earnest, upright life, had begun to doodle. But Celia was trying to put two feet under the table of each apostle.

"Twenty-one, I only have twenty-one. Of course its impressionistic and you have to compensate for the erosion of the stone, but I like feet to come out even," Celia said, exhibiting her one-track mind.

"I suppose my cardinal sin when it comes to women is sloth," said Peter, exhibiting his one-track mind.

"You know, that's very refreshing. Everybody I know claims lust for his or for hers."

"You're certainly entitled to have more than one cardinal sin! You're entitled to have seven! What the hell, you don't have *any*," Peter protested. He felt his lust ought to have gone without saying.

"Yes, I do!"

"You're just riddled with virtue, a sink of fortitude and temperance!" There was an edge to Peter's voice. He thought she shouldn't get off scot-free.

Celia was surprised and hurt, but kept her sang-froid, did not cry out. Instead she said firmly, "I have a monumental sin. The sin of pride. I don't like to follow the crowd. And since *everybody's* got a lover . . ."

Fifteen

Nᴏᴛᴡɪᴛʜsᴛᴀɴᴅɪɴɢ their inattention, or indeed the lack of evidence of a popular uprising either in the empty marshlands or the enclosed fields, Celia and Peter were brought to discover that the French revolt was growing and the strike spreading. Provincial airports and key train terminals, among them Marseilles, Nîmes, and Avignon, were shut down, as Peter read in a day-old *le Monde,* and so, once again, was the National Telephone and Telegraph Syndicate. There was no way to warn Agnes, therefore, of Celia's arrival that afternoon. Daunted and irresolute, Celia anyway ordered an advance. Giving Nîmes a wide berth, they headed west, off the map of Provence and on to the map of Bas Languedoc, and at midday packed their lunch on an unruined meadow under a lowering sky, in the middle of rough vineyard country. Pushing up over the edge of the horizon was the Cévennes, the southern range of the Massif Central, presenting a barrier and a harsh warning even from a distance.

"Maybe you better tell me something about this mother,"

Peter offered, in an effort to stay the metamorphosic confusion going on in Celia. Before his eyes she was shrinking from a youngish butterfly to a caterpillar.

"Well, as mothers go, if you can believe what you hear, mine is an anomaly. She asks *nothing*." Celia jarred her own nerves by the *nothing*, set her jaw and looked blankly about.

"My mother asked nothing," said Peter, thinking to give Celia's misery company. "She passed the years detecting slights, only so that she could forgive them."

"No, you'll see. Agnes is never a martyr, not if she can help it. She is the first to assure you that she does *not do* what does not suit her. Being a wife, being a mother did not suit her. She was born with a truly selfish nature which she saw as a gift, and from which she thought she would make an art, and even an ethic. And it's worked very well. She acknowledges all her faults in the most highly principled and in fact winning way. And then you can take her or leave her, you see. And it is always a matter of the greatest indifference to her which you do."

"And people stay away in droves?"

"Oh, on the contrary! She holds a court! People clamor for the privilege of attending her, young and old. She's commanding. You'll see. And she was quite beautiful."

"She didn't marry again?"

"No."

"But there were lovers."

"It's the sort of thing one doesn't precisely know about a parent," said Celia, a little tart. "There were *protectors* . . . and as a matter of fact the two men she's with now in Quissac, Robin East and Nick Allison—they've been her loyal friends for years. But hardly lovers."

"Is that Nicholas B. Allison, the composer?"

"And Robin is a cellist. Our Nell is going to study with him in London next year. Anyway, they've lived together in—how do you say?—a *liaison* that's long-standing. I've known them for quite a while. They stay with us in New York. They're very nice. English, but they've retired down here for half the year. I think it's a vineyard they've bought. Anyway, a lot of people are attracted to Agnes, although . . ."

"Although?"

"Well, they're discrete entities, these people. They're a sack of marbles . . . they don't make a fabric. They don't weave. They don't entwine. . . ." Celia paused, and heard an old rhyme in her head: " 'Feel where my life broke off from thine/ How fresh the splinters keep and fine/ Only a touch and we combine.' Browning. When Philip was young he knew a lot of Browning . . . it was very nice. . . ." And then to set the present matter straight she added, "I don't mean they're *all* queer."

But Peter only said, "I hope he's got beyond Browning."

It wasn't thirty kilometers between the meadow they left and the one outside Quissac that bordered the property they were looking for. At the edge of a woods there was a muddy road that led in, weaving and rutted, dipping down into bog before it rose to run along a wide hillside where vines were terraced. About a quarter of a mile along there was a U-turn that brought them downward to what was virtually a tiny hamlet, on the one side the large barnlike buildings of a working vineyard where everything was colored purple; the walls stained waist-high, dyed baskets of woven reed, dyed wooden barrels, and above all, the earth, soaked in purple deep into history, it might be.

Across the narrow road was a long, low tenement of gray stone where evidently the workers lived. There was nobody about, and they continued on a little further until they came upon the main house. It was of a comfortable size, not grand, settled under the shade of old trees, and of a French provincial design, of all things. It was a sight for American eyes.

"Oh, I *love* this. I *love* this," said Celia in a husky voice, more stirred by an almost modest domestic setting than she had been by the spectacular scenes Peter had led her to before, or by Peter himself. When he had at dinner in Aigues-Mortes watched her mop up her sauce with such an earthy joy, he told her he'd fallen in love with her. She had looked up at him thoughtfully, the joy a little spoiled, and said, "Well, I love you in my fashion." The husky-throated emotion—that was evoked by an old house.

It was Agnes, properly amazed, who answered the door.

"Celia! My *darling!* What are you doing here? I told you not to come!"

"Well, after all, you look *fine*," said Celia, immediately unstrung.

"Why not? All I do is rest, and the fever's gone."

Agnes looked fine. She was a tall woman, her angular frame softened by shawls in the reigning purple. She was of an uncertain age made further uncertain by a dribble of strawberry blond curls, arranged in the Roman fashion, and a powdered face smudged by mascara, and eyelids painted greenish blue. Celia stood before her in a skirt and sweater, her own hair tied back with a thin black ribbon.

Agnes said, "*I* look fine. *You* look fine. I don't understand how you got here! Who is this man? Have you left Philip? Now we've got to be quiet because from three to

five they do their yoga or something—Robin and Nick—
so we'll get some tea and you can tell me *everything*. Come
along."

Agnes talked on, in a deep attractive voice. Although she
was reared in Kansas City, she spoke the Queen's English.
They tiptoed over the tile floor of the vestibule, through
the cool dapple-green air of the high-ceilinged rooms, tall
windows to the floor, large Kokoschka-like paintings on the
white walls, to a comfortable kitchen, a kettle whistling on
the range. Agnes, knocking tea out of a tin into a teapot,
her head turning back and forth, talked steadily. "What did
you do with your hair? You know you look a *great* deal
better. Robin's going to be absolutely boggled. Here you've
come all the way from the States and he says they won't
even let you out of Arles! Sylvie, you remember Sylvie?
Well, she lives in Arles and she's coming for the weekend,
but he doubts she'll turn up. I mean there's simply no way
of getting any news now because they've *stopped* delivering papers and they've *blacked out* the telly. And *no* phone.
Of course we're used to that. There's only the padre.
I know what it is! You've put on *fat, that's* what it is!
Imagine!"

It was not possible for Celia to find equal footing. With
the first blast she was thrown backward into an early un-
confidence. She answered literally a selection of her mother's questions, identifying Peter as a historian, a friend of
Philip's and Tennie's—Tennie had published his books on
Italian intellectual history. Agnes's eyes traveled over Peter
while she listened to Celia, if she listened to Celia, and then
she said to Peter, "Well, I suppose it's you she has to thank
for a breather—pulling her out from under that *overlord*,
if you take my medieval meaning. Do you know what I

think, I *think* our padre has read your book on Italian communes . . ."

"There are a lot of books on . . ."

"But I like *you* and I want it to be *yours.* However, I must warn you, because he'll come by, he likes to think he's a *scholar,* and we agree to overlook his personal metaphysical problems. Just a minute, I think that may be Robin coming down. Wait until he hears you *can* get out of Arles. He really hates Sylvie. He thinks she's insane."

"Ordinarily she is insane," Robin intoned as he walked into the room, "but she has lucid moments when she is only stupid, if I may paraphrase Heine. How *are* you, my dear Celia? How *nice.* You're all right, are you? The children? Philip?" Robin East greeted Celia with a hug and a kiss for each cheek, as though he were sincerely pleased to see her. He was a man of middle height and comfortable bulk that fitted well against a cello. He had a homely, bulbous face, a lot of yellowing white hair, a foulard at the neck, and wore thick glasses through which he squinted to see what was and was not exquisite.

"I'm Robin East," he continued without pause, shaking Peter's hand. "Delighted. What a fine surprise. And how nice to have our Celia shepherded through this . . . *really* I think things are going to get a lot messier before. . . . There are *peasant* rallies, you know, just west of us, blockading the roads. I would certainly hate to think of Celia having to clamber over . . . all by her*self.* What have you got there, tea? We need a little whiskey. Let's have some whiskey." He had the highest regard for the civilities himself, and the lowest expectation that he would find them in others.

Robin led them into the living room. The rain had finally

begun to come down, swiping the long windows in gusts. Above were the banging sounds of a piano. Robin turned to Peter to pump him, while patting himself for matches to light a fire, and then filling a pipe he lit that. Celia watched and prepared a French sentence about pipes, the stuffing of them, the knocking into ashtrays, a vocabulary derived from the habits of Inspector Maigret. She did not deliver this sentence. She was not expected to hold up her end of any conversation through the ensuing days.

The sounds of the piano stopped, and soon after Nick Allison came down. He had been warned of new guests and had time to disguise his frustration. He disguised it somewhat. He told Celia she was a marvelous surprise and to Peter's How-do-you-do? he responded with a sort of good-natured bitterness, "So, the Americans are the last best hope, are they!"

"This blow-up has been a damned nuisance to Nick. He blames it on you people, on your war," said Robin, in ironic explanation.

"I just don't want you to forget, Robin, *you're* the one wanted to go to *California*, all-that-sun," snapped Nick. "At least *here* we have no illusions. It's the war of all against all. You wouldn't believe," he now addressed the Americans, "our *peasants*. They're out of Balzac! The padre says they've joined the strike, blocked the roads to Montpellier. He's an ass. They haven't *joined* anybody! Incapable of it. Out for themselves a hundred percent. Not the merest rudiments of fellow feeling in those black souls."

"Poor Nick's petulant because the young fellow who was to bring the proofs of his new concerto from London *can't land*," said Agnes, not very sincere in her commiseration.

Poor Nick was a short dark man, burly and bowlegged,

who might have come out of the coal pits of D. H. Law-
rence. He was a blend of roughness and refinement, with
nostrils that quivered elegantly. They quivered now. "And
according to the padre, the students, those poor benighted
babies, after they've pleaded and begged and *shamed* the
craven workers to get off their collective bottoms . . . do
you know they've not only shut down the Metro, they've
taken over the *Opéra* and *Opéra-Comique!* Total paralysis!"

"Of course, *I* don't like it," said Robin, with a wink at
Celia. "It isn't *my* sort of revolution. To my *Marxist* mind
it hasn't got *class*."

"Robin has ideas above his station," said Agnes. Her lap
was covered by a large work of needlepoint to which she
gave most of her attention. She was catching words on the
fly and embroidering them.

"The padre says the workers have told the students they
may not march into their factories," continued Nick, un-
daunted. "Well, of course! My God, that's the last thing
they want—an excuse to call in the riot police and have
their own heads cracked open! It's a war of all against all
'blindly stumbling after the something something god of de-
struction,' that's what Herzen said!" Nick was deflecting
his annoyance at the arrival of unexpected guests.

" 'If the contemplation of the universe fills one with
despair, it is the part of wisdom to think of something
else'—that's what Bertie said—somewhere," said Robin
sharply. And then he added in a pleasant voice, "Think of
the bright side. We've been spared Sylvie. She might even
be the victim of violence, although heaven knows not an
innocent victim."

"Don't be silly," said Agnes offhandedly. "Her son's

probably sent the children down from Paris for safety. She's very family-minded. She likes to take care of people."

"Agnes does not like to take care of people."

"No, I don't," said Agnes between her teeth. She was biting off a thread.

Sixteen

WHAT were once the stables at the back of the house had, on the ground floor, been restructured acoustically for Robin and his cello. Above that studio were two connecting bedrooms forming a private suite and given over to Celia and Peter, with a curiosity on the part of Agnes whether they would need only one. Either way, she was bound to be disturbed. That Celia was skipping off with another man would have relieved a certain wholesomeness she found in her daughter's personality, but by the same token, it would have alarmed her. It would have put Celia and her children in jeopardy and have distracted Agnes. She would have to think about them, worry about them, which she was not in the habit of doing. The doubt harried her.

"Sweetie, is this thing with Peter *une amitié amoureuse* or is it *un amour de tête?*" She had asked a bit cute the moment they were alone.

Celia was slow to answer. She had first to catch the meaning of the French and then her mother. It was clear that with the truth she would forfeit an unprecedented interest she had aroused in Agnes.

"Don't tell me," said Agnes, taking the silence for an admission. "You know, *I've* never been one to believe the moralistic side of one's nature should patrol the private passions."

Celia did not tell her mother that gripping her in bed these nights was the Simenon.

Sylvie never did show up, but the padre, their bearer of bad tidings, came round at eleven every morning for elevenses.

"Well, de Gaulle's tootled back from Romania. Told the students 'La réforme oui, la chienlit, non.' That'll straighten them out." He was privy to news nobody else got and kept them posted on the progress of the revolution, delivering his dispatches with amused disdain. "It's gotten quite bad, actually. Mother's Day's been postponed." For a padre he was in some respects disappointing, neither picturesque—no soiled soutane—nor even French. In fact he was a Scotsman in a Shetland sweater who had earned his sobriquet in the British army, and who had entered the ministry, according to Agnes, because it was the only way for a poor boy to get out of that working class.

"They've started to hoard, and overnight there's a tremendous black market," he said. "Well, get a good plague going and you'll never be short of rats to carry it." He was on pension for a disability and was down here working on a book about worker priests, he said. He was a spy, according to Agnes.

In spite of these bulletins on the fate of France, "almost total paralysis" was belied by reality in Quissac. Certainly there was no evidence of food shortages, nor did the vineyard workers appear about to rise in protest. Nonetheless, they were preparing to do just that on Friday, as the woman who came to cook warned them. That Celia was stranded was certain. The padre got a message to Paris for relaying to Philip: FINE BUT STUCK CELIA.

Agnes had always been deeply disconcerted by the arrival of Celia, from the day she was born. As she explained to Peter the first night, "I had reservations about the advisability of my being a mother, and after considerable thought, I acted on them. Morris, Celia's father, had the parental temperament. Celia's her father's daughter." And as an afterthought, "He had a noble character. That's where she gets hers." She had repeated this before Robin: an error.

"Your mother grudges you your character, my dear," said Robin to Celia. "You're the only one I've seen who can rouse something like *compunction* in her."

"Do you think I'm troubled by remorse?" Agnes asked, surprised and with a laugh at something so far from the fact.

"No, no," said Robin. "Remorse is what you experience *exclusively* when you let something slip away by inadvertence. No, not remorse. I think you're troubled by *love*, my dear. You love your child! Life's wickedest trick! So shamefully sentimental, but one of those things. . . ." He delivered this as a parting shot and left the room.

"These homosexuals! What a breed! They really think they're *chosen people!* They're worse than the Jews, worse than the Americans," said Agnes, ruffled, and with a darting look at Peter the Jew. "They're all brag," she went on. "Nothing makes them madder than Freud. It simply *infuriates* them, the idea that creativity is rechanneled sexual energy. Oh, how they hoot! *Nobody* has the sexual energy they have, and, mind you, of such a fine order! But what they really want you to know is that they don't *misuse,* they don't *dissipate* that extraordinary expression of their rare genius on *reproduction!* On the fathering of children! *You're* not a homosexual, of course?" she asked Peter, suddenly, checked by remembering that she had not quite secured the information about his relationship to Celia.

Peter laughed but did not say yes or no.

"Well, don't you think I'm right?" said Agnes, persisting, meaning to get the thing cleared up. "I mean 'Algeria, the best place for bed and boy!'—if I've heard it once! 'I have found those who do not like tobacco and boys are fools!' If I've heard it once! Jonson, Shakespeare, Leonardo, Michelangelo—what a roll call! How they *preen* themselves! What an elect!"

She prodded Peter for some sort of declaration, but Peter only produced a companionable chuckle, and in the meanwhile Robin came back into the room. It seems he had been listening. And he said with lofty condescension, "The original mind *tends* not to reproduce itself. I don't say *never.* And of course there's a very *low* correlation between fag and family."

Celia found herself terribly embarrassed but Agnes said, as though further vindicated in her criticism of that breed by evidence of their tendency to eavesdrop, "I don't hear Dickens on your list, I don't hear Dostoevski!"

Robin began to laugh; Peter had been laughing all along. Agnes narrowed her eyes at her miserable daughter, and in fond support said, "You don't have to blush for five children. Tolstoy had at least five children, probably more."

"I love Celia. She knows I do," said Robin. "I couldn't love her more if she were my own daughter!"

"I love Celia. She knows I do. I'm just glad she's not my daughter," said Peter, still laughing, and amused to confirm Agnes in at least one of her misassumptions.

Relations between Celia and Agnes did not remain so stilted as they had begun. In fact, there was a clearing of the air after this small explosion, and for the first time in their joint history they united in a sort of comic alliance. This was because Agnes was beginning to find her hosts annoying after three weeks of intimacy, and she was looking about. What she found to her surprise was an interest in Celia, deriving mainly from that misassumption that only one bed was in use above the stables. She was at first chagrined that her wholesome matron of a daughter had the nerve to manage an illicit fling so deftly, so coolly. It cast a shade on the elegant management of her own history. But then in an unusual rush of feeling her mother's heart swelled with pride at the crust of it all, and she struck an attitude vis-à-vis Celia that was for her quite hovering.

The days passed. The contrast was maintained between violent national events relayed by the padre—shutdowns, takeovers, barricades—and the orderly progress of the working days at the house. Late in the drizzling afternoons Nick led a trek through the purple mud, descanting on viticulture, darting here and there to pluck a weed, swearing at the absent peasants off blockading roads. ("Don't you think that's an . . . ethnic slur?" Celia ventured. "What?" "Peasants." "That's what they are, all right! Ethnic slurs!") But for most of the day, through the vacuum of hours set aside for composing and practicing, the house a trick box of echo chambers of moody sounds, Peter and Celia were silent in adjoining rooms. Peter, after a fallow period, had resumed work on a theme in Dante and often forgot about

Celia. And as for Celia, whether or not it was redirected sexual energy, she found herself deeply absorbed by the story of the fields and furrows of France. And unknowing, she took the first steps, in her chilly room by the electric fire, toward an enduring passion ("What mad pursuit! Cold Pastoral!")—the reading of great history.

Then one morning, Celia and Agnes, both bent over needlework by the living room fire, were talking about the children whom Celia was beginning to remember and miss, and she said offhandedly, "Well, I suppose it isn't such a good idea after all, sending Nell to study with Robin."

"Why not?" Agnes asked sharply.

"I only mean," said Celia in a reasonable voice, "it may not be the kind of household one ought to send a young girl into."

"You certainly knew all along what kind of household it was!"

"Good grief, Agnes, you're the one who cast the *lurid light*—all those boys!"

"Well, I must say I don't think that's very fair! Surely *you* were reared with impeccable moral tone in spite of an incredible turnover of Japanese houseboys! Would you say your divine father ran a brothel?"

"Agnes!"

"In fact he did. Or what comes to the same thing. You *can* be a *prig!*"

"You mean the uncles?"

Agnes now felt she'd gone farther than she meant, and she said, in a huff, as if she'd been pushed there, "You don't think I would have left you to wallow in depravity, do you? That unnatural a mother I'm not!"

There followed a silence of uncomfortable duration

which Celia broke by saying, in a mild, ironic voice, "Well, you've given me something to think about," and she got up and went off to do that.

Now it would be seen whether her long training in accommodation, instilled from earliest days by her dear father, by these very uncles, could be stretched to cover a little depravity. Could she make proper allowance for a nether side to her gentle but somewhat Edwardian childhood? She headed off past the barns, rounding the hillside, out onto the village road, Nick's old wide-brimmed gray fedora pulled down against the drizzle. She walked in a self-conscious attempt to feel the drama of this revelation. Logistically, it was clear at once how the trick was turned; always the east wing of the house out of bounds. Pushing on to the village, conscientiously, Celia recalled the uncles and brushed against the memory of her father. All the way back to the vineyard, however, it was the memory of her father plain; this fine, responsible, noble man, who had taken care of them all—against the dissolution of the family fortune, and always mindful of the needs and longings of each of them. Had she overesteemed him? Or had she not in fact underesteemed him, never dreaming of the variety of some of these needs and longings?

The walk lasted nearly two hours, through which Celia was not really emotionally wrung. What would certainly have shaken her twenty years ago, even ten years ago, was now too dated; crowded out by the richness of her own subsequent history, by Philip and the children. She got back to her room above the stables, feeling, oddly, lighter, as though she were finally rid of a too sweet version of her past; and unexpectedly very homesick. And feeling less sweet had the effect of equalizing things in relation to her mother, of achieving a parity with someone alongside whom she had been too clean before. She was not made upset by Agnes, for once and a wonder.

Agnes had made herself upset (for once and a wonder). After a term of conscientious sparring, she capitulated. When she heard Celia come back, she went upstairs to see her. Celia opened the door to her knock, and Agnes said, "I feel rotten."

"Oh, dear! What a mother you are. Don't feel rotten! I just don't want you to include my father specifically in . . ."

"Ach! I wouldn't even *know!*"

"Well, for the rest . . . a hill of beans . . ."

"But I feel rotten." Agnes stayed for a little comfort and reassurance. She did not need a lot.

Later that afternoon Celia told Peter that she wanted to go home, and he said, rather enthusiastically, that they ought to take advantage of the break in the strike, and even if there were no flights from Marseilles, she could drive on to Milan with him, leave from there.

The next day, after the happiest of farewells, they left. On the drive back Celia sang a great deal.

"Do you remember on that Beatrice Lillie record the song she sings to Maud?"

"No, I don't think so," said Peter.

" 'We're all of us, we're rotten to the core,' she sings to Maud.

> Dahling look at *you*
> And the sordid things you do
> And the sordid sort of people you adore.

"It goes on through several stanzas and then the last line is, 'We won't be rotten, dahling, anymore.' It's very funny. I wish I could remember more of it . . ."

She kept trying.

Part Three

❋ ❋
❋ ❋

The Good Fall (1976)

Seventeen

EIGHT years were to pass before Celia got to Dante, let alone Chaucer. Of course she had not frittered them away. She was well launched into the third third of her life and in fact all that remained was to keep it glorious. On her return from the trip with Peter, her first move had been thoughtfully to design an itinerary to the learned world. She set sail and immediately foundered. Then, inspired by those above-mentioned eastern saints who got into barques trusting to the winds, she gave the lead to what she read; and passed the years wandering highheartedly through history, all over the centuries. Unlike Odysseus she had no firm destination. Unlike Penelope she was not besieged by suitors. But she did a lot of needlework.

Although it was true, as Tennie had warned, that she would be relieved of all the economic and social functions previously ascribed to motherhood, he had not warned her that in the free time ostensibly provided by having none of these historic things to do, she would become foolishly vulnerable to an obsessive concern for the happiness of the five adult daughters. Yet none was being hung by her thumbs somewhere. Yet they were all feminists, albeit flawed feminists, as was their mother; and even their father. Yet each of them was off "realizing her potential," although none would have used such a phrase after life with such a father. But the spirit in these girls would droop. A sign of the times. In America, all the citizens not already resolutely committed to narcissism or schizophrenia (a clear majority) were turning to depression. This spring just passed the Dupont family had sat in a row under an awning at Bryn Mawr College to watch "Isobel Wendell Dupont of New York" receive her diploma: Bess, the fourth daughter to graduate, unsettled which way to go, whom to go with, and for how long.

Jane Austen's Emma was concerned that her friend Harriet was not reading, not improving her mind, and hence "not making mental provision for the evening of life." On that score Celia could not of course be faulted, but by 1976, it was a question that had completely gone out of fashion. From Emma's view the evening of life—beginning at forty had there been actuarial tables in those days—would find Harriet confined to a chair by the hearth in a married daughter's house with nothing to occupy her mind; an unwelcome nuisance and no help in a household into which children were being born, brought through crises, catechized, taught their letters, *taught their manners*. Celia, however, at fifty-three, while finding terrifically profitable the mental provision she had made for the evening of *her* life, was nonetheless regularly disconcerted by the absence of these grandchildren about whose manners she was prepared to be very stringent, and the unsettled future of some of those who ought by now to have been their mothers.

She had been all set, she had been in place, the ancestral house had been ready, the time ripe for the generations to continue their unfolding. No one threw the switch.

The decade did not send these daughters into actual jeopardy, as it did some others of the people in Celia's life, although nobody was outright dead. But counterindications to the whole idea of the best being yet to come were beginning to proliferate. Of course, to intend a glorious third as well as to sing about happy endings it is better to have a taste for Brecht than Browning. At the end of September, after Polly had begun her freshman year at Carleton College in Minnesota (the three younger girls did not choose Smith—talk about rebellious youth), Celia joined her mother and Nell at Quissac, where poor Nick Allison was in a wheelchair, following a stroke, while poor Robin's fingers were attacked by arthritis—he was ordered by his doctor to wash the breakfast dishes in hot water every morning, he who had never rinsed out a glass. They would have to give up the vineyard and return to London. This was an inconvenience to poor Agnes whose year was a selective peregrination, like a Royal Progress, bringing her to Quissac for a month in the spring and a month in the fall. Agnes was otherwise almost hearty from watching others falter. At home Tennie had had a heart attack.

The girls were not in jeopardy, but for instance Nell, who was twenty-six and who had been living in a lonely, underheated room in London studying the cello, eking out her living with lessons and odd jobs, announced with beaming face to her mother at Quissac that she had been awarded a grant to study at the Institute of Archeology (London) to train to become a conservator.

"And give up your music?"

"Of course it's not just a whim, mama. I've thought a lot about it."

"Good grief! You'll be thirty before you're out of school!"

"*All* learning does not have to be deferred until middle age!"

But on the other hand, Francie, now twenty-eight, was deferring hers. She had found another woolly mammoth, in Cambridge, Massachusetts. They were having a Relationship, and she had stopped work on her thesis. Woolly Mammoth II had himself dropped out of graduate school to become a carpenter, and although now making a fortune building bookshelves in a shop on Brattle Street he called Library Science, had yet to win the hearts of Philip and Celia. When he and Francie came home for a visit they were given separate rooms. For that matter everybody's relationship was given a separate room, although nobody's folkways changed on this account.

So the time had been ripe for the unfolding of the generations, and then overripe. One fall day after Celia's return from her latest visit to her mother she had said to herself in effect, the hell with the ancestral house. This was in part a measure of how far she'd relaxed her hold on her reverential caretaking of the family history since Agnes had introduced a doubt about its affecting innocence, and in part the tripling of the price of heating oil since the Arab embargo.

"I've got a terrific idea. Let's sell this place and move downtown," Celia said to Philip, who was entirely unprepared for such a thought in his wife's head.

"You're crazy! You don't want to sell this house! Your father was born here!"

"We could ask Marian and Tennie to keep their eyes open for something near Washington Square. I'd like to be walking distance to a university library."

"You wouldn't have your garden! My God, you've just separated the iris!"

"With Polly off and another room closed, it's like living in Kafka's burrow."

Philip's two protests were *pro forma*, and in a minute he was working out the asking price. Every one of the five daughters, however, said it was out of the question. Harriet, in particular, a second-year medical student in Chicago with an interest in psychiatry, was fearful for her mother's mental health. Each of them told Celia that her father was born in that house.

"*You're* the one who's always had such a belief in the ongoing generations!" Francie argued.

"But you don't get *on* with it!" said her mother.

"And what about your philosophy of family, of a house, a private life!"

"I'm *revising* it!"

It may have been the winter closing her into a dark house with the thermostat at 62°—God knows what Celsius —but Celia had been experiencing a little crisis of confidence that made her vulnerable to the helpful criticisms and suggestions of others. Of course, in her dogged pursuit of learning—she went after Proust the way Ventris had gone after the decipherment of Linear B, and it took her nearly three years—it was natural that she would occasionally droop with fatigue; and that from time to time she should suffer from a boredom with herself and with the unrelieved need to be the sole generator of her intellectual growth, the sole beneficiary.

That joy in the life of the mind is subject to undulation is a solemn truth. Still, success is inevitable. To borrow an analogy from *The Divine Comedy*, once you are past the gate into Purgatory, you are destined for the sublime. There's no escaping. Outside you may shuffle and delay, be sullen, be stalled by pride, envy, anger, sloth, gluttony, greed, and lust, but once through, while the way is arduous, the prospects for moments of ineffable joy are certain. The pilgrim Celia found herself fundamentally changed and delivered in the nick of time from the embarrassment of being an aging ingénue. She was amazed by her own accruing wisdom, felt finally fully grown, and more, that her life was "worthy of being lived," in those words of Proust that leapt from the page. And if she had dragged her heels at the end of Purgatory, unable to proceed joyfully with Dante to Paradise, it might have been the shock of meeting Beatrice and hearing nothing but reproach:

Look at me well. I am she. I am Beatrice.
How dared you make your way to this high mountain?
Did you not know that here man lives in bliss?

Once it was determined to sell the house Celia more or less careened through Paradise getting right through to the bliss.

A calm followed Dante before she began her next great pincer movement. In it she was reading a spellbinding history of eighteenth-century France in which all the extensive and fascinating footnotes were in French. Here may be the place to note that an autodidactic experience with languages is full of surprises. It might be thought that by the end of Proust one would know as many words as the French knew, but there are areas Proust did not really

cover; the moral fiber of people who are affected by rainfall, as Peter had once put it, and its attendant vocabulary:
drought, dearth, scarcity, impoverishment, rising prices, infanticide. Countless times Celia had to turn to the dictionary to understand a program initiated by the Church, in
the years before the Revolution, to arrest the increase in
infanticide, to save the souls of unbaptized infants. It seems
a carter was sent off from the Foundling Hospital in Paris
for a three-month tour of the provinces. He pulled a small
tumbrel through a route of villages and hamlets and was
authorized to offer a few sous for unwanted *baptized* infants. Each infant wrapped in rags was placed vertically in
the cart to save room, a bit of wine-soaked rag in its mouth.
Between villages those that died were flung by the way to
leave space for new. It was not a perfect system. The
carter returned to Paris with a cartload of live infants, a
bounty on each living head. The archives record that in
forty-eight hours in the neighborhood of 2 percent had
survived. The problem of unwanted infants continues to
resist solution.

One morning while Celia was in this calm, Marian called.

"Listen, Celia," she commanded, "I've just got a minute
but I have three things to tell you. First, there's an apartment right on the square I think you should see. It's only
got two bedrooms and a maid's room but there's a huge
living room and a paneled library in let's-see-what-does-it-
say-here, *oak*, and it's on the third floor so of course there's
no skylight but it's silly for you to take up painting anyway. So I said you'd get back to them by the weekend.
And second, Tennie wants you to come *here* for Thanksgiving, and third, and this is what I really called about.
Lily's looking for a wholesome mother-type to lead a pro-

abortion lobby in Albany. Well, nobody *looks* better qualified so I submitted you. She wanted to know of course whether you could handle it, and I said sure you could, and you had the time. Now *think* about it. Don't just say no out of hand. Lily will be back here for Thanksgiving and you can talk. But I've got to know what to tell them about the apartment. Let's see that's one, two, three. OK, I'm going to run." Bang went the phone.

"No! Out of hand!" said Celia to her empty house.

The children spin off, the survivors huddle, and Marian and Celia saw more of each other in these latter days. They exchanged fond feeling, each in her way. Marian's way was of a utilitarian nature, and she thought a lot, evidently, about how better use might be made of Celia's time. But it was Jessie who fortified Celia's resistance to the thoughts other people thought she should think.

Jessie had in eight years divorced a doctor and married a law professor who was warm, sensitive, loving, interested in travel, theater, chamber music, walks in the country, natural food, and pottery. She had passed months studying the personal columns of several serious journals, consulting Celia about the wording of responses, and it is a testimony to the integrity of the winning periodical that the professor was all he professed. However, Celia, always dubious about the natural food, met Jessie frequently for a compensatory lunch at an Italian restaurant on Second Avenue, a moist and vernal bower where the hanging plants were fed organic nutriment and the customers pasta. Professionally, Jessie was a college student counselor.

About Marian Jessie said, "I told her to knock it off, get off your back. Your reading, your improving the mind, was actually an early form of consciousness-expanding. I said to her your doing all this thinking was for the *cause*, for the movement, so after the flood, this time, it'll be a *woman* . . ."

About Celia's daughters, she said, "It's not just your lot. It's *everybody*. You meet an old friend you haven't seen in years and the first thing you can't do is ask what are the children doing, case they're *pushers*."

"If Francie'd marry somebody with an attic, we could store our stuff."

"Well, of course if she doesn't marry she doesn't qualify for divorce. She's got to think ahead."

"These serial relationships . . . She just always seems a little depressed. I always hope to hear her . . . heart sing . . ."

"Anybody get depressed sleeping with one man after another. First they sleep with him. *Then* they ask are they in love? They got it ass-backwards. How can you fall in love without cultivating your romantic imagination, without giving it a lot of play, a lot of time? No wonder they're depressed."

"You know, the best, the richest parts of my life have been due to chance and to ignorance, and I worry that our girls . . . *know* too much, look too hard at things, and they won't stumble into dumb luck. I mean, for instance, they have no idea how much deliberate blindness, denial, blundering on, you need to make *anything* nice. You need a romantic imagination just to be willing to get out of bed in the morning. Take wanting children. . . ." Celia was sounding mournful.

"Oh, a lot of women still want children, Celia," Jessie said reassuringly.

"I mean *after* they have them." She told Jessie about the

tumbrel full of infants. Then she said, "You think, well, if the mothers could have *fed* them they would have wanted to keep them. No room in history *yet* for your average girl who says, 'I don't want them on *any* account. They're a nuisance, they're boring and dirty, and when they grow up they're not grateful, and they leave you flat.' Well who knows how old and fine that tradition is?"

"Of course, a lot of women *don't* want children also."

"Well, I know, some don't, some do, it's all the same— so long as you're responsible. That's received wisdom today. Only I really don't think it's the same. I loved having the children, even keeping them. I can't really honestly say to my own daughters, it doesn't matter."

"Listen, Celia, you ought to clear your head of those girls. Let them walk out on you, not make them look back. All you were ever required to do was toilet train them and see them through driver's ed, and you did that. Most people I know feel their real life only began when they'd shaken the dust from their feet, left home. I feel that way. I feel I only began to live when I married Eph . . ."

"Well, that's not so encouraging."

"In those days if you remember, you married to set yourself free. Of course your father set you free by dying."

"I don't see it precisely in those terms."

Eighteen

CELIA returned buoyed from her lunch with Jessie to find in her driveway, blocking the door to the kitchen, a Land Rover with a Vermont plate and a sticker that said, "I BRAKE FOR ANIMALS." On Celia's bumper there was Udall on the left and Carter on the right. The Land Rover belonged of course to Mary-Louise, who had not called first, who had let herself in, and who greeted Celia in her own kitchen after an absence of four years by saying, "You ought to take those stickers off, now the election's over. At least the Udall."

"You know what happens to me when I see 'I brake for animals'? It makes me want to *kill!*" snapped Celia, enraged at once.

"It seems to me when a president is finally chosen . . ."

"*Everybody* brakes for animals. It's *reflex!* I think it sounds so *sanctimonious* . . ." Celia stopped, recovered herself, and said, "You look wonderful, M-L. I don't think I've seen you look so well in years! What have you done? You've lost weight."

"You haven't," said Mary-Louise. "Listen, I've got a terrific surprise for you."

"What is it?"

"You know my mother's ninety-two . . ."

"That *is* terrific."

"But she really gets around and she says you're thinking of putting this house on the market."

"Oh, well," said Celia, flushing. "We certainly haven't settled on. . . . But the problem is heating it—the oil—and with just the two of us living here it . . ."

"You remember the money you lent me? I bet you thought you'd never see it again."

"Of course, now it's getting winter, and with the children gone, I've closed off a lot of the rooms and we've put this coal stove in the kitchen. But we do a lot of shuttling down cold corridors . . ." Celia continued, uneasy, and unable to protest that it wasn't only the money.

"I've always intended to pay you back, but what with the divorce and the tuitions, I had to reorder my priorities. After all you actually didn't need the money then anyway."

"I just forgot about it."

"You could afford to. Anyway now the kids are more or less on their own, and what with my position in the bank, I finally have my head above water, and here's your check. $6,500."

"Oh, that's too *much*. I couldn't take it! It wouldn't be *fair*."

"Seven and a half percent. It's more than fair. And you can use it. It means a lot to me to see the tables turned."

Celia took a breath, then bit her tongue. There was no doubt M-L had been sent to humble her, but by whom?

"The banking business is very challenging, and I have a feeling for it. I was always good at math, do you remember? And they reward merit. It's more than you can say about the church. There's nothing like a paycheck for your self-respect."

"It beats a life of Christian service."

"You think you're kidding. Anyhow, I've got some more news. You remember I told you about Bob?"

"The man you were having a . . . the relationship with?"

"We're going to get married."

"Oh, M-L, how *wonderful*, I'm so *glad* for you," said Celia, and threw her heartfelt support into a move that would excuse her from being troubled by M-L's fate. She listened gratefully, but she was not to be excused. "Do you ever hear anything about Cal?" Celia asked, after a while.

"Do I ever hear anything about Cal? He just *lives* in the next town! I hear *everything* about him," said M-L irritably, in a tone of rebuke, and then her eyes filled and she put her head down on the table and cried silently. The intensity of feeling caught Celia altogether unawares, and with a clumsy, but at least sincere, response to this pain, she tried to cradle M-L in her arms, stooping over her, putting her nose in the top of her springy hair to comfort. She was truly in awe before a mysterious providence that would plant the last of the steadfast hearts in a tacky soul. Mary-Louise talked and recovered. Celia, abased, listened.

"I don't worry about them," Mary-Louise said and meant, in reference to her children. She had volunteered this, but of course none of them was actually a pusher. About her older son she said only that he was an "alternative person." The younger was in the ministry where he introduced modern forms of expression such as singing to the guitar, and she sang, "A drop kick for Jesus through the Goal Posts of Life,'—that sort of thing."

"You're kidding."

"You mean you never heard that? It's very popular. Boy, you really don't know where it's at, do you!"

To be fair, she did not sound enthusiastic about what either of her sons was doing, but her daughter had earned her respect. She was a graduate student in psychology, was married, with a baby, and lived in Boston.

"They're into this theory that the father's just as important for the child as the mother? And they really trade off. Because they've discovered that statistically, even those women who want children won't want more than three, and figuring six months to nurse each child, that's only a year and a half the mother has to be out of work. Well, I guess they're not going to stay home and take what I and you took!"

"I bet you're crazy about that baby, though," said Celia, who had a bad attitude about statistics.

"Oh, he's just adorable, but I don't get to see him too much. Once I'm married, it will be different, but I don't like to have them over when . . . in another man's house."

"My God, he's only six months old. How could he know you're living in sin?"

"You'll probably think I'm foolish but actually he's the real reason I've decided to get married—for appearances. An old-fashioned reason."

"Oh, I *don't* think you're foolish," Celia said warmly.

"I'm still carrying the torch for Cal. That's the truth. I always will. But frankly, I'm one of those highly sexual people. I need that satisfaction. I feel I'm entitled to it."

At the end of the visit, when M-L was actually going through the door, she turned around and said, with good nature, "You know you're the only woman I know not working? I guess you're out of synch." She laughed, her joke.

"Oh, well, I did make a sound investment," Celia answered, a frozen smile, good to the end.

Mary-Louise retained the knack of reducing Celia, making her be small.

She was still being small that evening when she said to Philip, "Don't you think it's a little odd that nobody but Jessie thinks I take *seriously* what I'm doing?

"And me."

"I could see why people wouldn't give a damn *what* the hell I was doing, but they act as though secretly I run a vacuum, if it was only a brothel! Everybody wants to get me out into the real world."

"Not me."

It was after dinner, and they were in the library where there was a fire. Philip was sitting with his long, slim legs crossed, the trunk of him much enlarged in eight years, and his face a hearty, healthy pink from high blood pressure. Celia was not herself proving to be one of those women of uncertain age who sacrifices her face for her figure, another of Proust's observations that gave her a timely boost. But it didn't last. She needed another now:

"M-L says I'm the only one she knows not working, not earning a living, but if I'd gone back to school like Jessie, become professionally trained, had a first-class job, you know what I'd be now? I'd be so *unhappy*. I'd crave to be free to come home and read. This sort of steeping into the world of learning—you know, you've got to be *old* enough to do it well. It needs a seasoned mind . . . and then everything that goes before seems to become an apprenticeship. . . . Funny . . . all the knocking about, the passions, ambition, rewards—if you can get through all that, if the girls could only see it will all be worthwhile in the end when they finally get into the calm, and can be detached, observe, read, *think* . . .''

"You know the girls do believe you've put middle age on the map," said Philip in a comforting tone, willing to associate himself with that position.

"Of course *Marian*—she seems to feel any woman who *thinks* betrays the feminist movement," Celia went on, still prickly.

"Well, she's a political activist. She can't afford to stop and think or nothing would get done," he said in a soothing tone, to no avail.

"I can't talk to any of these women. If somebody says to me 'What are you up to now?' and if I say *The Iliad*, if I say there's a new translation of *Iphigeneia at Aulis*, they think the only reason could be that I'm documenting the history of male dominance. But Aristotle says all men naturally desire knowledge. I didn't think it up. It's scarcely an original idea, and now they've extended it to women, you'd think they'd cheer me on! Do you want to know what I've discovered?"

"What?"

"That it's just as unpleasant to be bullied by women as by . . . anybody else."

"Well, and of course your father was reading *The Iliad* again when he died," Philip said, with the intention of shifting the subject.

"Yes! I forgot about that. Isn't that funny? I forgot all

about it," said Celia, and this caused her to muse quietly and restored her better nature. "You know what reading history is?" she said, all at peace now, "It's disarming. It makes me feel less combative. Have you noticed?"

"Most of the time."

"I think it's because the passing of the generations is so rhythmic, so organic, that it makes our own deaths *accept-able . . . fitting. . . .* Do you think that's macabre?"

"Just a little."

Now Celia felt all recovered and had Philip's standing-by to thank for it. She did not think to thank him. It must be put to her discredit that although Philip had in fact evolved, become something larger, with a spirit that had taken up "greeting," a change that ought to have been gratifying to her antideterministic beliefs, she did not quite notice. That is, she recognized that he was gentler, and intellectually more accessible, and she was even able to lay the happy change to her memorable outburst that eve of her departure to France. It had set Philip on a friendly course, she thought. When she'd gotten back he appeared oddly re-lieved, oddly appeased, and so, more or less, he continued. He had thrown his whole weight behind Celia's glorious third, got interested in Proust, began to read a little history, a little poetry, switched from Browning to Hardy, and never again forgot a book list.

"You know what Churchill said about his wife?" he asked a little later, in an affectionate voice, breaking the silence. "He said she was incapable of an ignorable thought."

So far had he come.

Nineteen

O<small>N</small> the very evening Philip had put himself in mind of Churchill, he had casually referred to another subject with which he had never really made his peace, and which in fact had caused him to respond to Celia's sulkiness with more soft answers than were warranted.

"Funny thing," he said a little awkwardly. "Had lunch with Tennie today and happened to mention a new book on Vico we want to review. By Isaiah Berlin. It's evidently first-rate, and we're looking for somebody able to handle it. He says Peter Jacobs is back in town. Did you know that?"

"Oh, yes, but he's only here for two weeks." Celia offered no more information on Peter, as was her habit. She thought that her husband in his random tossing-off manner was tossing off Vico, not Peter Jacobs, and that he was demonstrating his own capacious range of interests, with this now easy embrace of an arcane scholar. Philip had become a kind of sage himself, with a syndicated weekly commentary on the American culture. It was witty, perceptive, and drew heavily on his wife's mind.

But Philip was tossing off Jacobs, not Vico. He wanted to hear that Celia didn't know Jacobs was in town, had no interest in him any longer, and that the affair was finished.

Just as it had not to this day crossed Celia's mind that Philip had been seriously involved with Lily, so Philip never doubted that his wife shared more than board with Jacobs the weeks in France. Why else would she have returned home as though stamped new, as though freshly validated, and with such girlish and irreverent airs? It may be argued that he assuaged his own guilt by discovering a reflection of his own ebullience. Whether or no, he had been very shocked, had had terrible difficulty adopting a sauce-for-the-goose, sauce-for-the-gander frame of mind, and it is possible that if it weren't for the explosive (and intimidating) egalitarian rhetoric of Women's Liberation, he would have found it beyond his competence to live in silence with the knowledge of Celia's liaison. As it was, the strain made him a feminist. This was a giant step for Philip and although painful, was profitable professionally, and moreover was catalytical to the recharging of his long-coasting mind. He probably never could have become a sage without this liberation. But it was against his grain to extend his support of equal rights for women to Celia's equal right to stray. It was a largesse that never set well with him.

"I bump into him now and again. He seems so *passionate*, so exuberant . . ." said Celia, after quietly following her own train of thought.

"Peter?"

"Vico. I'd like to read that book. I remember the first time I'd ever heard him mentioned. You know who told me about him?"

"Peter?"

"Lily. It was the time you and Tennie had that wild matchmaking scheme."

"Maybe *I'll* read the Vico. That's what I'll do. It'll certainly make material for a column."

Celia did not hear Philip's dodging the subject of Lily. What she heard was his scurry to appropriate Vico for his own, which was uncharitable, and refraining from comment, she went back to her book. But by and large, and notwithstanding Celia's lingering habit of defensiveness toward Philip, they had become the most comfortable of aging couples, and thought they knew each other inside out. They were right about 90 percent of the time. Ninety is high. Only in China and Albania would you get 100.

Had it been up to Philip, the word "Lily" would long since have dropped out of cognizance in his house, but Lily was not a born receder. To see her through Philip's eyes: she had no more than migrated to Massachusetts and settled into her new job when she discovered herself repressed, along with half the citizen population, and with her rosy flair and her pragmatical nature was able to tease the money from several gentlemen of means, Philip among them (because, she said, there weren't any sugar-mummies) to launch a really mean and snappy weekly newssheet for intellectual feminists. It was called *Bottom Line*. It was immediately a great success—Philip's loan was paid back long before Celia's was—and the kind of people who knew what International Woman's Year was all about, not to mention the kind whose sister-in-law had a paying job with the National Organization for Women, were bound to hear Lily's name a lot.

Philip's affair had continued an intermittent course, conducted by Lily at rare intervals, with a certain unrenouncable carnal joy, but no love to be lost, and the intervals grew wider in part because the aging lover was felled by a series of illnesses, a back operation, and high blood pressure. Philip did not quit altogether, however, until Tennie had a heart attack in '72. As for Lily, she had always expressed an enthusiasm for what Philip could buy, what could be done with his influence and loose change, and when he made his parting bow, she was refreshingly free of regret or gratitude. The thought of her now inspired in Philip merely a sentimental feeling for his old weakness and the proof of his old prowess. He never thought to see her again. Fate, however, was planning a reunion.

As to Peter, Philip was wrong about him from start to finish. Celia's score was a great *A*-minus, although when people gave themselves lustful airs—when Mary-Louise confided her overriding needs in this line, for instance—Celia thought with some resentment that if chance hadn't turned up Peter—if it had sent along Jawarharlal Nehru or George C. Scott or MacNeil-Lehrer, she might have gotten a straight *A*. Few people are satisfied with their final mark.

Two separate but equal things happened to Peter in Italy in the years following his sojourn with Celia. He ran into his first wife again, and he began worrying about his stomach. At first tentatively and then with a rush, he determined to combine his preoccupations by remarrying Marina so that she could cook for him. Celia had egged him on. They lived in Rome with a son Marina had added in her interlude, but once or twice a year he would land in New York for some lectures, seek Celia out, sit her down, and have her listen to all his thoughts on the above two subjects.

Quite understandably Celia had anticipated the first few

visits with immense excitement, sure that she could delight him with her new learning and her willing ear for his work in progress. But Peter had become rapidly uninterested in a breathless Celia full of thoughts. He wanted a confessor. She struggled—she still struggled, but his will was stronger. When in town he stayed at a hotel on East Seventy-seventh street in order to be close to the archives at the Metropolitan Museum. It was there through the years, for lunch or tea at the cafeteria, where he could see what he was getting, that Celia was kept abreast of his small circle of domestic concerns.

Celia had gone to Kennedy to pick him up, watched him come through customs, not old, still nimble, in a muffler and raincoat and a worried smile. She saw at once that he was tired and she could get her licks in; about finishing Dante, and the proposed move to the Square, about not only heading for *The Iliad* but doing it in Greek, a project that should take the rest of her life. She said she was so glad he'd come because she'd been waiting to ask him the greatest favor—nobody had his clout—would he get her clearance at the downtown Institute Library? "It's an armed camp! They won't let you through the gate."

"No problem," he said. "I'll bring it next week." And they arranged to meet when they could really have a good talk.

They met at the Museum cafeteria on an early afternoon at the end of the following week, got a carafe of white wine, which has fewer calories, and found a couch to loll on at a table right on the water.

"One thing about me hasn't changed," he said smiliing. "I like to be with a good-looking woman. I have to hand it to Marina. She's still got a lot of style."

Celia decided to take it for her compliment.

"I'll tell you what's on my mind," he said, changing to a brisk tone. "We want Geno to come here for his university education. Columbia. He would start his freshman year in September. . . ." And then he looked at Celia, his expression softened to the old look of love, and he asked her, "Do you know *why* Columbia? Because *you'll* be near. He'll have you and he'll be all right." And then brisk again, "He really doesn't want to come to America. We're being very firm."

"I'm not at *all* sure it's wise to *force* . . ."

"The Italian universities have become madhouses, and frankly, I'm anxious to put some distance between . . . he's got a sort of *incestuous* relationship with his mother. It will be good for him to get out of the house. I've assured Marina that he'll be right up there near you . . ."

"We're going to *move*. Do you remember I said that we're moving? Down to Washington Square? Just a small apartment. That's why I wanted the library clearance."

"Of course, there's always my brother and sister-in-law but they're both working and they refuse to be bothered with this sort of business," said Peter, searching his mind a little and not coming up with an alternative.

"Oh, guess what!" Celia said, in a voice of false cheer to cover a rising frenzy. "Philip's got a book on Vico for review. He was wondering if you—"

"I haven't a minute."

"I said you didn't have the time, so I've begun it. It's captivating. How passionately he knows that one must *will* a great leap of the imagination to understand what it's like to be somebody else . . ."

"Of course, everybody understands it now, but he was certainly 150 years before his time."

"Not *every*body."

Trying again, a little while later, she said, "Do you remember, Peter, when I first met you and you introduced
me to history by saying I'd be fascinated by the role of
rainfall? Well, I've run into an interesting connection between rainfall and the French Revolution, and scarcity and
the problem of infanticide, and I immediately thought of
you."

"Oh, I don't want to kill Geno, I just don't want him
in the same country." A joke. Celia pushed on with the
French peasants and the carter, and Peter's face took on an
increasing expression of concern. Finally he said, "I wonder
if that mayonnaise was all right? Suppose we walk a little."

When they were saying good-by, and Celia reminded
him about the library clearance, he said, "Jesus, I forgot.
I'm so sorry. I'll tell you what. If you pick me up on Friday
and drive me to the airport, I'll have it for you."

Twenty

THANKSGIVING was to be at Marian's and Tennie's, and the first reason for this was that none of anybody's young would be back from Nepal, Colorado Springs, London, or wherever. The second reason was Tennie's death-defying turn to cooking. He had taken to heart trouble with an amazing enthusiasm. The doctors told him to cut down, so at Heavensgate he did, but he was not a true believer, to his great glory. He devoted the newly available time to the art of French cuisine extending into the Vietnamese, a kind of defiant gastropolitical statement, as it implied an abundance of sugar, salt, fat, and starch, and meals preceded by champagne so as not to disturb the palate. He appeared very happy on his fatal course. Tennie certainly wasn't the only husband to trundel out into the kitchen, so many wives having gone off to work. Without the men, God bless them, there would be far less good food offered at far fewer dinner parties.

Philip and Celia drove down to Washington Square confident they would find no parking, but they had an awakened interest in circling the neighborhood, and Philip said, "Of course, we'll get rid of the cars. Just rent when we need one. Save a fortune." Already he felt a better citizen.

"I'm not entirely sure your plan to pile four girls in the maid's room looks *hospitable*, suppose they all turn up at once," said Celia in a happy voice, as though game to try it. They both liked the apartment Marian had found and were now both excited by the prospects of change.

Tennie and Marian lived on West Third Street in a narrow old apartment building, the back bedrooms giving out on airshafts, winter or summer receiving very little of the light of day. The compensation was the grand front room, full of books, a remarkable number with the Heavensgate colophon, of small gold-patterned carpets Tennie collected on a dark wood floor, and shabby furniture that Marian did not have repaired. Now it was a pretty haze of lamps and chatting guests and great yellow chrysanthemums sent by Celia. Jessie was among the guests, taken in because the children of the marriages were with the fathers. And standing with Jessie and Tennie, in the middle of the room, looking like a portly but well-to-do gypsy, and waving an empty champagne glass in greeting was, unmistakably to Philip, Lily. This was a big surprise to him.

"Ah, Philip love, your wife is just the woman I've come to see," said Lily in a voice easily heard above other voices.

Philip was immediately made nervous by the familiarity. He feigned a mild pleasure in his greeting, and the courtesies were exchanged. Celia could scarcely see a vestige of the bouncing girl she remembered and thought Lily looked much taller and stronger, the effect of the Afro hair and the long, heavy gold chains she wore, and fingered, and might have broken with her bare hands.

"It isn't only *you* I want," said Lily in her hearty voice to Celia. "I've got a challenge for Philip too. I want him to do something *really* bold. I know he has it in him. Philip the Bold," she said, giving Philip an ironic look, laughing, and turning back to Celia. "It's this lesbian thing. We've got to have broader support. It's pulling us apart. What we're looking for is a heavy, an authentic straight. And well, talk about ramrods, I can testify for Philip, and with his new column planted right in the middle of Total Woman turf. . . . Actually, I think it's your obligation," she said, turning back to Philip.

Philip scowled, shifted about, and said, "I'll just go and see to our ration of champagne. We don't want to ask the Lord's blessing without our champagne," but he didn't go.

"I was wondering," said Celia, "whether a moratorium on the subject of . . . *erotic choices* . . . wouldn't be in the best interests of women."

"I believe I ought to warn you, Lily. Celia is really kinky about sex. She thinks it ought to resume being a private matter," Jessie said this to protect Celia.

"Celia does *not* subscribe to the let-it-all-hang-out school of thought," said Philip, to protect himself. Tennie brought their champagne and Philip drank his down.

"I'm sure you're not *naïve* about sexual politics," said Lily to Celia. "*Temporizing* is hardly a luxury we can afford. The fact is we have to hammer away until the issue of lesbians in this country is confronted as frankly as rape, abortion, divorce . . ."

"What a roll call! A new Jerusalem!" Tennie said, already a little drunk. It was after all his champagne. "You're really a romantic, Lily. Did you know Lily was a romantic, Philip?"

Philip the Bold ventured nothing.

"I think there should be a terrific fuss about abortions," said Celia, stiffly, pricked by the political language.

"My God, you can't be against *abortions*," Lily exclaimed, looking about to see if she was in Peoria by mistake.

"No, but I certainly think abortions should involve shame and anguish."

"Celia's worried about your ridding the world of mental suffering," said Tennie.

"I'm worried about ridding the world of *mental content*." Celia set her jaw and then added in a hurt voice, "I don't like to hear women sound so . . . shallow. It's a great disappointment."

Philip saw Celia's jaw set and assumed a stoical look.

Jessie said, "I am always being embarrassed intellectually by our group. It grieves me to extend my sense of betrayal to your . . . yellow sheet."

"The fat's in the fire," said Tennie.

"Well, then, let's eat," said Philip.

"I'll tell you what I think, Lily," Celia said. "The feminist movement has been marvelous for men, and for middle-aged women, but . . . to the young, to the instinctive *passion* and *generosity* of the young, it offers—day-care centers. It recommends *deadened* sensibilities. I really think *Bottom Line* could be the advocate of a feminism that is . . . *noble*."

"You don't have to deaden the sensibilities of a twelve-year old inner-city kid knocked up by her mother's boy-friend!" Lily shot back. She was of course a militant.

"*That* kid doesn't read *Bottom Line!*"

"It may help you, Lily, to recall Celia is the mother of five daughters," Jessie said.

"Well, five daughters or no, I don't see how you can expect us to send you up to Albany *quivering* with *compunctions!*"

Marian, who had brought the turkey to the table and was trying to get her guests seated said impatiently, "Oh, for heaven's sake, Lily, don't take her compunctions so seriously."

"My God! Turkey!" Philip bellowed. A heartfelt, desperate bellow. "I'm simply delighted, old boy, it isn't heron or whooping crane," he prattled to Tennie. And he was even more delighted to see the provoked Lily placed a tablelength from his provoking wife.

The festive meal proceeded, the fellowship expanding, the sisterhood subsiding, and Philip relaxed his guard. A lot of wine was drunk. But then, in the détente before dessert, while the men, sated and hazyheaded, were recalling army life in World War II, a comedy of inexhaustible interest to the original comedians—suddenly without warning, Lily said, "Listen, Celia, if you think sex ought to go back to being a private matter, you haven't learned much in ten years about the political realities." Lily made this a friendly observation.

The old soldier Philip was back on guard.

"I know I may sound quaint and unconvincing if I take myself as a point of reference, but I do not want to hear about other people's sexual activity and I don't want them to hear about mine." Celia was friendly too, not testy at all.

"Well, dearie, there's no tactical way to avoid the lesbian business, but the idea that we could be *noble*, I like that."

"I think it's real catchy myself," said Jessie, also in good humor.

"For instance," Lily continued, now wearing her editor's hat, "I'm thinking about the five daughters. Now frankly I don't see you in Albany, but . . ."

"Why are you going to Albany?" Philip asked Celia, confused.

"I'm not going to Albany."

". . . but for a format, say you're a *mother*, now what do you want to see for these daughters?"

"Well, first of all I want to see them set very *high* intellectual standards for themselves, and then—well, I guess the rest is luck."

"You mean if they can hack it in a man's world?"

"I mean whatever else they also do, if they're lucky enough to provide a haven for themselves with books, and maybe a husband and a couple of babies. Someplace where they could retreat, where they could grow . . ."

"Celia believes a housewife is somebody who teaches herself French so that she doesn't have to depend on a translation to read Proust," said Tennie.

"Don't be silly, Tennie. I don't think they all read *Proust*. For heaven's sake, there's the whole history of civilization!"

This was all, of course, banter, but it wasn't pulling Lily's Noble Feminist piece together. "That's awfully elitist," she said doubtfully. "How can we tell women to stay home with the baby so they can read the history of civilization?"

"No, it's more complicated. You haven't got it right. The only elite is the elite of elders with wisdom and experience—of whom there are too few today to . . . put on the graph. No, if you're going to restore nobility to feminism, you have to begin by restoring the dignity of a private life, regardless of whether or not a woman works. Of course she doesn't have to read and have babies. I only wish to note that in my experience it is a good combination."

"Just for the record, there's another point of view," said Tennie to Celia. "Sartre has an interview in *le Nouvel Observateur* where he says that he knew when he was about nine years old that he had a great work in him, and that he couldn't afford to have a child because it would draw from his intellectual energies. Well, he says, now, at the end of his life he sees that he was right. He didn't have the son and he did the great work." Tennie thought this was funny.

"Well, I must say that's shocking!" said Celia, and she looked quite taken aback. "And for a philosopher like Sartre, why it's almost *solipsistic*."

"Now do I call that a devastating rejoinder?" Jessie asked.

"Maybe that's the angle to take," said Lily, off on her own tack. "Sartre. Set him up and then we'll shoot him down. Of course, we've got to draw a convincing picture of all these women reading in the kitchen."

"Be great for the book business," said Tennie.

But Lily was quite fired up and took Celia into a huddle, and they made arrangements to meet in Boston on Tuesday to work on authenticity. They might do a series. It was an idea, she said, that would have a future for Celia.

When they were saying good-by, Lily said, "Well, Celia, I like you. You've really given me something to think about. Now what about you, Philip? What are the chances of your taking on the lesbians?"

Philip smiled, put his arms around Lily, kissed her warmly on both cheeks, looked at her wryly, and said, "Miniscule."

They left, and how they got out of there without any of the real beans spilling, Philip never knew.

Twenty-One

Tʜᴀᴛ night Celia and Philip had just fallen asleep when the phone rang. Waking to the phone could be the number-one killer before heart disease and cancer in this age group. It was Celia who answered.

"Hello," she said, a voice in command.

"Mama, where *were* you!" It was Francie, still alive.

"At Marian and Tennie's," said her mother, with some annoyance.

"On *Thanksgiving?*"

"Well, for heaven's sake, did you want us to keep a *lonely vigil?*"

"Now, don't be fretful, mama. I've got wonderful news! You know how you're always waiting for the generations to unfold? Well, I'm unfolding! Mama, I'm going to have a *baby!* So we talked it over and we decided not to get an abortion. We decided to keep it and get *married!* At *home,* at Christmas! You don't have to sell the house!"

Francie was breaking frontiers, and she wanted to be assured her mother was astonished. Her mother assured her she was doubly so, listened to her daughter's excitement, and recovered. The grandfather-designate then took his turn and Celia heard him say, "No, no, I'm delighted you woke us. It isn't the kind of news that keeps till morning." In fact both parents heard these glad tidings with excellent sportsmanship, as could be read in the proud strain of their faces. Afterward they couldn't sleep, put on their robes and went down to the kitchen to huddle by the coal stove with brandy. Both were very thoughtful, both uncommonly silent.

"So," said Philip finally, with false cheer, not wanting to force Celia's hand, "you're going to see another little creature pad about these halls after all."

Celia was finished with these halls and slow to answer. "You don't think we could pack it into the maid's room with the rest of the lot?" she asked smiling, uncertain.

"Well, I really *do*. It's little and it'll fit," said Philip with enthusiasm, relieved to hear Celia still resolute to move. However, he immediately saw that a grandchild of his would need more space, and after thinking about this he said, "I suppose there's always the possibility we've discussed—going in with Agnes to buy Quissac. There'd certainly be room for the lot of them there. I know it's a little out of the way, and it isn't ancestral . . ."

"Wouldn't that be ironic, Agnes installed as the grand matriarch? Serve her right."

"My God, your poor old father would certainly be surprised to see her take on the family duties."

"My poor old father . . ."

Again they were silent. Then Celia, who had resumed brooding about Francie, said, "I wonder if I didn't sound *enthusiastic* enough. I mean I'm really *glad* about the marriage and the baby, but the whole thing is. . . ." She drew a large breath, and to her own bewilderment, began to cry. Philip, who thought this was proper under the circumstance, patted her back and poured her more brandy. In a moment, Celia took up her sentence again. "I guess it isn't very motherly of me but the whole thing is a little *anticlimactic*. And the idea of keeping this house! I can't wait to be rid of it! But, of course, I wouldn't want her to know . . . I'd like to give her the greatest sort of support, that we're 100 percent for her, that bells are ringing . . ."

"I'll tell you what we'll do. We'll turn up the thermostat, put on a grand bang of a wedding, and then we'll clear out. How about that? I've got a good idea. What do you say we drive up to see her tomorrow? Then we can—"

"I *can't* tomorrow. I'm going to take Peter to his plane," said Celia. "But anyway, you know, Philip," she continued, taking his hand, grateful for his stalwart support, and wanting to reassure him that she was good and ready to get out of the castle, "You know, there's something I've never confessed to you. That trip in '68 when I was stranded in Quissac—"

"Oh, *don't*, my dear, don't. It doesn't matter. *Never* confess the past. You're the first one to say no good comes out of a clean slate." He did not want to hear about Peter.

Philip spoke so firmly that Celia backed off from her sorry tale about the houseboys, very willing to let it drop forever, and she only murmured, "Oh, well, you're right. It doesn't signify. It's ancient history. I only mean that the Webbs aren't all that spotless. They're not more entitled to be family-proud than the next lot."

"Family-proud," he said. "Do you know what I haven't been able to get out of my mind? That story you told me the other day about the carter and the baptized infants. Do you know that in the Jewish cemeteries in eastern Europe, the ghettos had so little land they had to bury their dead straight up and down? Well, and then I had a sort of Darwinian thought that our being alive at all means that through history none of the necessary progenitors was . . . put in a cart . . . that those of us alive today are an aristocracy, an aristocracy of survivors. Just to be here, it's a lot to be in awe of, enough aristocracy to suit, more than enough. I just thought I'd like you to know I was a born-again democrat, that's all."

"Ah, see that," she said smiling affectionately. "Well, you're smoothing everything out. Maybe you can . . . there's just one more thing niggling for me. I was wondering how you felt about it, but . . . I really don't want to get involved with Lily. I wish I hadn't said I'd go up there."

"I don't care if you *never* see her again!" Philip said, more supportive than ever.

"You know, I really don't like to let women down, let anybody down. . . . And Marian's right. I don't acquit myself . . . I'm not active. I don't make any money. I don't even jog. Sometimes I just lose my . . . sang-froid." She smiled.

"Dearest girl, what I've always admired about you is that you're *not* well-rounded! I don't count the actual new poundage."

"Well, then," she said, feeling much better, and suddenly interested in that grandbaby, "Maybe I'll just get out of taking Peter . . . all I wanted was that library permit and he's probably forgotten it again. But if I don't have to go up to see Lily next week, we could really go to Francie tomorrow."

The next day, before they set off for Cambridge, Philip said, "I've got something for you, a Christmas present, but I want to give it to you now. It's because you sometimes get discouraged about your poor memory—I found you a commonplace book."

He handed Celia a paper bag with the present not yet wrapped. It was a kind of college notebook, thick with empty lined pages, and covered with the sort of wallpaper they had in the dining room. The first page recto was blank, and in a large calligraphic hand there was written:

Cecilia Agnes Webb Dupont

and underneath, smaller:

These fragments I have shored against my ruins.

Celia was very moved. She couldn't find anything to say. Finally she murmured, "I forget where that comes from."

"*The Waste Land*. It comes from the end of *The Waste Land*."

"Well, that's really a coincidence, you know, because it was reading *The Waste Land* that finally set me on this path, the time Harriet . . ."

"Goddamit, it's not a coincidence! Do you think I'm likely to forget the day you took it up to read. Nothing was ever quite the same after."

"Is that what you remember?" she mused dreamily. "Well, I love that, Philip. You know I've got the first entry for this book . . . I'd like to show you, although . . . although it may seem a little tacky under the circumstances." She looked at him doubtfully, and then said, "You shave and dress, and I'll go down and put it in."

When he came down, she handed him the book and said she would go out and warm up the car. He read:

Personal relationships seem to me to be the most real things on the surface of the earth, but I have acquired a feeling that people must go away from each other (spiritually) every now and then, and improve themselves if the relationship is to develop or even endure. . . . We are more complicated, also richer than we knew and affection grows more difficult than it used to be, and also more glorious.

E. M. Forster

DATE DUE